MALKI PRESS

Cyclops from the Forge

Stephen Toman

Published by Malki Press, Edinburgh.

Copyright © Stephen Toman, 2020

The right of Stephen Toman to be identified as author of this Work has been asserted by him in accordance with sections 77 and 78 of the Copyright, Designs and Patents Act 1988.
All rights reserved. No part of this book may be reproduced without prior permission from the author or publisher.

This book is a work of fiction and therefore any resemblance to real persons or situations is coincidental.

ISBN: 9798643220671

Cyclops from the Forge

Stephen Toman

Ghost Eye squats by the fire. Flames dance with the trees, flickering on the wood, on the bones that hang from the branches. The cabin stares from its glassless black windows and door. Ghost Eye pulls strings of slimy meat from a metal skewer with leather fingers and pokes them through the slit of its mouth.

The snap of a twig makes Ghost Eye stop and turn in the direction of the noise. It puts down the skewer, stands up, skin creaking loudly as it uncreases, stops breathing and listens. Ghost Eye draws a revolver. The leather of its elbows squeak. Ghost Eye holds the revolver by its thigh, waiting. When the man bursts from between the trees Ghost Eye shoots him in the gut six times. Before he even has the chance to complain about this, he is dead. Sausages slop out from his two halves like from a burst paper bag. Barely a man. A boy, really. Somebody likely put him up to it. In his open eyes the expression of fear and pain and relief all at once are drawn on them like paper. Ghost Eye leaves him there to become bones like the others, decorations to disperse like talismans or carried like streamers by animals.

Ghost Eye climbs into the hole, pulling the soft cool soil around itself until only its head remains above ground, lets the fire burn out.

rattlesnake shake

THE MAN STRUGGLED FOR BREATH, stopped with his hands on his knees, bent over, gasping. He took off his hat and used it to fan his face. He straightened up but then dropped suddenly to his knees, retching. He wiped his mouth with his scarf and sat back on his heels.

Behind him on the ground lay a body wrapped in a blanket. Strapped to his back was an axe. He stood and collected the bundle in his arms. It was about a third of his size. He cradled it against his chest as he walked out beneath the empty sky towards the centre of the plateau.

He closed his eyes, stood there swaying. Then he put down the bundle, kicked away some stones, some bones, like he wanted her to be comfortable, like she would notice these lumps on the ground. Then he unwrapped the bundle and lifted first the legs and then the shoulders to retrieve the blanket. Without stopping to think about what he was about to do because he might not have been able to do it if he did, he spread out the dead girl's limbs and took the axe in his hands.

When he finished, he scattered the carrion. Then he dropped to the bloodied dirt and buried his face in the blanket, thinking he could smell his daughter on it, the way she smelled when she was still alive, but he knew that he could not.

It was dark by the time he opened his eyes.

The scavengers had arrived to take the girl from this life.

He stood up, turned away from the sight and made his way back down the mountain.

Of course when the agent found the remains scattered like the pieces of a jigsaw puzzle he thought there'd been a murder and, though it made him vomit several times, and he did so with tears running down his face, salt streaks drying on his cheeks, pulling limbs and other bits from the beaks of vultures, collected what he could and bundled the girl into his sleeping sack, which he then slung onto his horse and led it down towards the camp. He was not a young man but he was strong, he was fit. He repeated this to himself like a mantra.

∞

The girl's father was handcuffed to the leg of a bed. He sat on the floor, his hands behind his back, eyes red. Before him, his daughter was in a pile on the floor. The agent had emptied his sleeping sack like he was pouring coal on a fire. Now he sat in the chair composing a telegram. Some people could be heard sobbing in another tent. His sleeping sack hung on a line outside.

Do you know where I might send a telegram? he asked the man on the floor.

The man, having just that morning dismembered the body of his only daughter and had therefore already gone through the worst experience of his life, only shook his head.

I thought there might be a place nearby is all. Seems like a big construction job like this might need of a place.

Still the man said nothing.

You mean you don't know of a place, or you know that there isn't one close by?

The man closed his eyes.

The agent made a noise like he was farting out his face hole and the smell of his breath was not any more pleasant than if it had come from his back-passage. He licked his teeth. They were rough with plaque. He once woke during the night to the foulest smell, thinking he had shat his pants but it was just his breath. He had been sleeping with his face tucked into his arm, which he'd been using as a pillow, and his exhalations had collected in his armpit.

I could send a letter, he said, making that noise again. But how long would it take to receive a reply? I can't leave you tied to a bed for what could be weeks. Months?

He pondered this.

The girl's father was not worried. He was surprised to make it this far. He reached for his daughter's remains with his foot and toed a bit of her, he didn't know what, it was all a jumble. He was not angry at the man, though he should be. He raised his head.

What are you going to do with this?

Those? The agent wiped his face on his sleeve. It hadn't crossed my mind. A burial, I reckon. Return her to the earth. The circle of life, isn't that what they say?

He drew a figure of eight in the air.

The girl's father let his head drop onto his chest.

Are you smiling, sir?

∞

The girl's mother should not have screamed.

The agent had nodded off polishing his pistol, but when she burst into the tent with the knife she had taken from the mess held high, screaming, he woke and shot her in the chest before he even had both eyes open. The girl's father flinched at the noise but otherwise did nothing. The knife dropped to the dirt. The woman did too.

Well shit, said the agent, looking down at the two bodies, if what was left of the girl could be described as such. Would one refer to ground beef as a cow? Even a whole one? Now he just felt sorry for the man. Though the girl's father deserved to be punished, this—the death of his daughter (even if by his own hand) as well as his wife—would be too much for any person to be asked to bear, so he pulled the trigger and placed a bullet between the man's ears, though it came to rest elsewhere. Then he puffed out his cheeks like he was playing a trumpet that wasn't there or he was fellating somebody.

Ah shit, he said eventually, deciding to leave rather than stick around to explain the three bodies on the floor, one of them in bits, to whoever came to investigate the gunshots, who likely knew the dead folk and would take their side, even if he was the law, which didn't always count for much in these parts.

At the entrance to the tent he stopped with his gun drawn to see if there was anybody about but the railroad camp was a noisy place and it didn't sound like anybody had heard. He took one last look at the heap of limbs on the floor and shook his head. Who could do such a thing to a little girl?

THE TRAIN LINE ENDED when the tree stumps did, a little ways beyond the camp. The workers were felling them to clear a path for the track and using the same lumber to construct it a section at a time. When a length of track had been laid down, the locomotive would haul the workers and their equipment to the end of it and they would start on the next section. If they were within hiking distance by the end of the day, the workers would return to the camp. On longer days they would pitch tents—just a sheet of oiled canvas and a stick to hold it up—and when they got too far out the whole camp would be dismantled and loaded onto cars and the locomotive would haul it all to the end of the line where they would construct their little town again. Some folk stayed behind, decided that they had more or less settled and set about constructing more permanent lodgings for themselves, hotels and brothels and inns and saloons and schools and haberdasheries and so forth.

The trees to be cut down had a white ribbon tied

round them. Figuring the planned route might lead somewhere, the agent stuck to it, touching each tagged tree when he came to it, looking behind him every now and again, which had become a habit.

∞

He hitched his horse by the door. A sign above it read, THE RATTLESNAKE SHAKE. A handwritten notice in the window said, *Try our Rattlesnake Shake.*

What's the Rattlesnake Shake? he said to the bartender. Does it have anything to with the line to the crapper out back?

The bartender's mouth was hidden by a drooping but well-groomed grey moustache. A cigar poked out from below it, so there must have been a mouth in there somewhere. His eyebrows could have come from the moustache of another, lesser, man, and the agent was tempted to ask him about this—Say, are you cultivating those eyebrows as a moustache on behalf of a man struggling to grow his own?—but couldn't figure out the right combination of words for it to function as a joke.

It's our specialty, replied the bartender, pronouncing it *spe-shee-al-ity*, even though he pronounced the word *special* as *spe-shall* and not *spe-shee-al*.

What is it? A drink or something?

It's a drink.

A shot or—

It's a shake.

Like a milkshake?

Ci.

Is it good?

If you like bourbon. It's our specialty, saying it that fancy way again.

Alright then. One Rattlesnake Shake please.

Ci, said the bartender. Please . . . He pointed with his whole hand towards a table. I will bring your drink to you.

The agent thanked him and sat down. The tavern was surprisingly empty but for a few other patrons. Maybe they were all queuing up out back.

By the time the drink came the other drinkers had left and were replaced by different ones and the agent had read every bit of writing he could see, signage for customers, a chalkboard menu, another advert for the Rattlesnake Shake, and posters advertising a travelling carnival and one for an evening with Obediah Crow, the Mountain Man.

It's pink, he said when the bartender put the drink down on the table.

Ci.

It came served in a tall glass with two straws protruding from the white foam.

I wasn't expecting it to be pink.

It is pink. Like the snake.

The man hissed.

Rattlesnakes are not pink.

They are pink on the inside.

What came first: the name of this place or the drink?

I don't know. Please try.

The agent took hold of both straws and sipped. It tasted like bourbon and milk.

Tastes like bourbon and milk, he said. And something else I can't put my finger on. Something astringent . . . Bitters?

When he woke he discovered he had missed the show. The Mountain Man Obediah Crow, was at the bar. Two men were speaking to him, asking him to repeat or elaborate on one of the stories he told in his show, and the Mountain Man Obediah Crow was happy to oblige, at least until the drink they had bought for him had been drunk, at which point he stopped talking, mid-sentence, and didn't say another word until another one was placed in front of him or his glass was topped up, and he would pick up exactly where he left off.

—*brain boils inside of his skull till it popped and pink soup came spilling out . . .*

He looked more or less exactly like his illustration: chest-length beard that stuck out like bristles on a broom, hair plaited down his back like the tail of an Indian's horse, the hollowed out face of a bear upon his head. His skin-coat hung over the back of his stool.

The agent beckoned for the bartender.

Did you like your milkshake, sir?

I can't say that I did. But, then again, I can't say that I didn't. That might have been the best sleep I've had in a long time. Might have preferred to have it somewhere more comfortable, however.

Would you like another? Stronger, perhaps?

Stronger?

It would need to be. Your body has become accustomed to the venom.

The venom.

From the rattlesnake.

I'll have a whisky.

Of course.

The bartender went to go.

Hey, amigo, the agent said.

The bartender turned.

How much for that? He gestured towards the poster.

A dollar?

The bartender took the poster down from the wall and rolled it and brought it to the agent's table along with a whisky. The agent gave him two dollars and left a couple more coins on the table. He felt his feet sticking to the tobacco on the floor. His vision blurred.

You looking for someone, friend? said a voice behind him. Its owner spat.

Peanuts. That's what you need. Bowls of them on the table, let customers drop the shells onto the floor, soak up some of the spit, the tobacco, spilled beer, vomit, piss, blood, and whatever else.

He did not linger on the men watching him. One of them had a hole where his nose should have been. It was not commonplace but it also wasn't the first time he had seen a person with it. Frostbite was the usual culprit, though round here the man was as likely to have lost it in a game of cards.

He collected his hat from the table and nodded at the men on his way to the door.

∞

He dug in his pocket and counted the coins. Not enough for a room. He needed to send a telegram, get some money his way.

Fights in the taverns spilled onto the horse-shit street, piano keys clanking from behind swinging doors. Whores offered themselves to him, spat tobacco onto their porch when he didn't respond, or said, See ya around, handsome, if he smiled and said, Maybe next time. When the town was nothing but a collection of flickering orange dots behind him in the dark, he turned off the path and ventured back into the mountains.

He took his blanket from his horse and unrolled it onto the sand.

Another night out here, he said. Sorry girl.

His stomach growled.

Should've eaten at the tavern. Shouldn't've drunk rattler poison.

He chewed on a strip of dried deer he'd bought from a tracker a month ago or thereabouts. At least, he'd been told it was deer.

He lay awake and looked at the stars. He did not

remember falling asleep but when he woke the three men from the tavern were standing over him and his nose hurt something terrible. He touched it and felt gristle move beneath the skin.

Hands where I can see them, partner.

You can't see them on my face?

In the air, smartass.

The agent put them above his head. The man who was speaking had a rifle pointed his way and a black hole where his nose used to be. The man's companions stood behind him. They also had guns but left them holstered.

Can I help you boys?

Shut it, old man.

None of them said anything while they eyeballed one another. Then the agent whistled.

You want me to roll out a tumbleweed? he said. Make this encounter seem more dramatic.

You think you're funny, old man.

I thought so. But, in truth, all I got's the same handful of jokes I just repeat in different circumstances, much to the vexation of my poor wife, who was there for most of them.

Where's she now?

She's dead.

What'd she die of?

She died of suicide.

On account of your jokes?

The agent lowered his hands and clapped politely.

Well done, he said. You got that one.

Then he winked.

The man with no nose turned to one of his companions. He was older, taller too, with the gnarled, bony face of someone for whom food was merely a source of fuel, lank hair straggling from beneath his hat.

I think he's trying to make a fool of me, the one without the nose said.

He sure is, replied the older one.

Reckon I should break his nose with the fat end of this rifle?

I don't reckon that's necessary, Thrush.

I don't see what harm it would do.

That what happened to you? the agent asked.

Got hit in the face with a rifle? Thrush touched the black hole with a finger. Naw, mine's just fell off.

Sneeze too forcefully or something?

Something like that.

Listen, said the older one, stepping forward. We got a proposition.

Who are you people?

The older one helped the agent up.

We're bounty hunters, he said.

Who you hunting?

Anybody that needs it.

That's mighty fine of you.

See, the thing is, we could do with the law on our side. Someone with a badge.

I'm retired.

That so?

That's right.

The agent climbed onto his horse, made a point of adjusting his rifle as he slung it over his back.

I sure am sorry I can't be much use to you fellas. He touched the brim of his hat. Then: Whelp, best of luck to you, gents.

Thrush peered down the barrel of his gun.

Want me to shoot him, boss?

Let him go.

You sure? Because I really feel like shooting him.

No.

Last chance. He's getting away.

I said no.

I still might hit him from here. I've done the same distance before. If you want me to, I mean. I might miss but it's worth the shot.

Go for it then. See if you can hit him with the gun in your mouth.

Aw, I see.

They watched the dust rise behind him. It never settled, just hung there. Only time it settles is when you breathe it in and it coats your throat, your lungs, and then you cough it back up again.

On his way back to town—might as well find a place to drink if he was going to be awake all night looking over his shoulder—he saw the posters in the store windows, pinned to telegraph poles, fences, advertising OBEDIAH CROW: THE MOUNTAIN MAN and some other ones that said MISSING GIRL above a line drawing of said girl. It was too dark for him to read the name as he trotted past but he allowed himself a satisfied smile knowing that, even though he would not have been able to recognise the girl in the picture, not from the bits she was in when he found her and probably not from the drawing either, that he got the perpetrator. Probably the one that did all them others too. Their posters hung in a variety of conditions, curled and faded, monetary rewards scored out and larger amounts scrawled below, some of those scored out as well and replaced with even larger sums, and others just scored out altogether.

∞

Another shake?

I don't think so. I'll just take a straight whiskey this time.

I can give you the venom as a chaser if you'd prefer. If you found the milk unsettling.

No, I don't reckon it was the milk. Thank you.

He took a seat.

The bartender brought him his drink.

The agent leaned back in his chair, against the wall, let it lift his hat off his head by the back of the brim.

You're in luck.

I am?

The show. He gestured towards the stool on the stage. On the back of the stool hung a coat of skins, which the agent recognised from earlier. The evening performance is about to begin.

Well isn't that swell.

Obediah Crow, the Mountain Man, took to the stage from behind a curtain and sat on the stool. He leaned forward as he spoke, one arm resting across his knees like he was stoking a campfire.

∞

I escaped by chewing through the leather thongs they had tied me with. I supposed they had never seen a man so desperate to escape. Then again, maybe I wasn't the first. There aren't too many men who could have seen what I did and not done everything they could to get away. A woman, maybe.

I would have gnawed through the iron bars of a jail cell if I had to.

What'd you see, Obediah?

They kept us in a cage during the day. In the baking sun. Beneath the pale moon, freezing, at night. Every day they'd take one of us out the cage. They'd torture and kill them in front of us.

What'd they do Obediah?

One man I saw they scalped him and hung him upside down over a fire and let his brain boil inside his skull till it popped and pink soup spilled out.

∞

A woman brought her fingers to her lips. A man vomited on the floor. A young boy's mouth opened and did not close again till the show finished.

∞

I'd've chewed through a brick wall to get outta there too, Obediah!

But that's not what got me.

Not even when they caught the pink soup in a pot and drank from it.

No.

What did it for me was the Dismantled Man.

∞

There was a commotion and some shushing from the audience.

Can't you keep it down?

A crowd of angry folk were trying to push through the saloon doors.

Can't you see there's a show going on?

Pipe down.

Hush, dammit.

The man is trying to speak.

Then it became apparent that the people at the door had weapons.

The agent opened his eyes. He wasn't asleep, just listening to the man speak, but it took a minute to register the disruption.

The man at the head of the mob had a rifle. He scanned the room and found the agent, tried to point the gun at him. The agent sat up and fumbled for the gun at his hip, struggling to draw it in the seated position.

A man stepped in front of the mob. Tall hat, checkered suit, business type. The mountain man's manager or some such. On stage the mountain man had disappeared. His skin-coat was gone from the back of the stool.

Next thing the man with the tall hat wasn't wearing it anymore but was wearing a hatchet instead, and the man with the rifle, if he was wearing a hat to begin with, which he wasn't, no longer had anything to wear one on.

Still the mob piled in amidst the ruckus, shooting, maiming, swinging fists, bottles smashing and all the rest, and the only man in the room with a badge ducked and crawled beneath the tables and snuck out without anybody seeing.

Outside, his horse was in bits. So he ran.

∞

He found the three men on the plateau, could smell their fire from the path. Two of them sat on their packs watching the flames, gnawing on ribs or thighs or wings, pulling the meat from the bones with their teeth and tossing them over their shoulders into the dark when they were done. The agent could hear dogs growling but couldn't see them. The third man was crouching over the fire. He looked up at the sound of the agent's feet crunching in the dirt.

Well look who it is.

His face was lit up by the fire, a black triangle where his nose used to be.

The agent was out of breath. Second time climbing to this same spot in twenty-four hours and, other than one or two brief periods of unconsciousness, he'd not had any sleep. He put his hands on his knees and tried to steady his breathing. He looked behind him.

Someone after you, friend?

It was the older one who said this. He did not get up.

The agent pushed himself upright, put his hands on his belt buckle. His chest rose and fell.

Seems that way.

Take a seat.

He put his pack on the ground and sat on it like the others.

Lost your horse?

Lost in the same way I lost my mother when I was ten.

Someone cut your mama into pieces? said No-nose.

I mean that it's dead. It was a joke. Remember those?

Hey, boss, he's starting his shit again.

Thrush, get this gentlemen some dinner. He gestured towards the spread beside the fire—a pot of beans, a plate piled high with meat on the bone, and a mountain of charred and broken johnnycakes. You got a plate?

The agent stood and pulled one from his pack.

Thrush here is a good cook. Never used to be but he's been practising.

How do you like your eggs? Thrush asked.

The name's Henrikson. The older man held out his hand. The agent leaned over, trying to suppress a grunt, and shook it.

Allan, he said.

I like my eggs like I like my victims—soft on the inside, said Thrush.

That'll do fine, Thrush, said Henrikson.

Thrush cracked four eggs in a pan and put it on the fire. Then he splashed a little whisky on it so it started to steam, passed the bottle to the third man, who'd not yet spoken or even moved into the light, and covered the pan with an upturned plate.

See? said Henrikson. He's learning.

After a few seconds Thrush stood, took off the plate and cleanly lifted the eggs one at a time onto it. Then he went round his three companions and slid an egg each onto their plates.

You fellas sure know how to make yourselves comfortable.

The agent took a hunk of johnnycake and used it to burst the yoke. He appeared to consider it for a moment, the eyes of the other men on him, waiting for a reaction, then he stuck it into his mouth and nodded appreciatively.

Must not forget the beans, said Thrush, spooning a heap of them onto the agent's plate. Some meat on the bone poked out from amid the beans. The agent lifted the bone and the meat came cleanly away.

And to think you wanted to shoot me, he said, looking at Thrush.

Thrush grinned.

Bone at the teat, he said.

There was silence while they ate. Though Thrush began last, he finished first, announced he was done by throwing the bone he had been gnawing on into the fire, washing his dinner down with a mug of whiskey, and tossing his bowl into the dirt. Then he belched loudly and farted.

The other white meat, he said.

Doesn't have to be white.

It was the first thing the other man had said. Until that moment he had sat silent and hidden in the darkness, his face shadowed by an oilskin hood. His voice was high-pitched, cheerful, enthusiastic even, particularly for a person without eyelids or lips.

The other three turned to look at him.

I'm just saying. It's a common misconception. I've had dark meat before and I didn't get the shits or nothing.

The agent pondered this awhile before sleeping. Not long at all, really, before the drink took him. The men, though he remained wary of them, were as generous with their drink as they were with their food. And they did not appear to be in any better a state of affairs than he. They seemed to like him. Or need him, at least.

LONG BEFORE SUN-UP the agent awoke, brain vibrating with thoughts only occurring to him now he was starting to sober up.

He had made it into his sleeping sack. A good sign. He was wearing the same clothes as the previous day. They were ripe, certainly, but this also was a good sign. His weapon was there too. His horse was not. This was not good but was consistent with what he knew to be true.

When he returned to the camp after emptying his bowels the other men were awake and eating breakfast. Another pot of beans on the fire, more meat. They turned when they heard him coming and waved. Henrikson patted the ground next to him.

You feelin alright there?

The agent patted his stomach.

Any of you fellas ever had a rattlesnake shake?

They laughed.

You had one of them things? said Thrush.

Sure did. I figured that if a place was named after a

drink then the drink was worth trying at least. Also, I didn't figure on it having rattler juice in it.

At least it hit your stomach out here instead of back in town. That shit would've cost you a hundred dollars in butt wipes, said Henrikson.

And you can't just shit in the street back there. They lock you up.

He's speaking from experience.

It's not something the locals drink, is what you're telling me.

That's right, said Thrush, spooning some beans onto a plate for the agent.

The third man had his back to the rising sun. His eyelids had not been torn off, that was clear enough now, in daylight. Skin peels, stretches. But this man's eyes looked like the lids had been hacked off with a shard of broken glass or a sharpened stone. Looked like he was wearing someone else's face. A death mask.

The meat in the beans was burnt black. The agent held it on the edge of his fork.

I bet you couldn't say what colour that was before it was incinerated, said the man with no eyelids.

Ignore him, said Thrush. This one I think was more of a golden brown.

The agent looked around for other signs of a hunt: drying pelts or rolled-up furs, sausages curing . . . What he was eating must have been butchered elsewhere.

You fellas camp out here often?

Thrush stuck out and folded over his bottom lip and tilted his head from one shoulder to the other noncommittally. The third man did not have a bottom lip to do this with. His mouth was locked in that same grin, all the way to his ears.

Regular enough, said Henrikson.

I thought as much.

Makes you say that?

The bones.

He waved his spoon at the dirt.

There's a lot of them. Either you eat here often or you butcher here. Either way, this is a regular spot for you.

You were here yesterday. Did you see us then?

You saw that?

Saw the whole thing, said Thrush, enjoying the way he said it.

Saw that poor man give his daughter a sky burial. Saw you scoop her up in a pillowcase and sling her over the back of your horse.

Saw you kill the mother and the father.

I saw that too, said Death Mask.

Don't those ever dry out?

These things? Death Mask touched an open eye with his finger. Sure they do. I just pour a little boiled water down the barrel of my gun and fire it into each eye. Usually takes care of it.

Twice a day he does that, said Thrush.

The agent nudged a bone with his boot. Half-buried in the red dirt, it could have been a pork-rib or a turkey leg.

The other white meat.

More of a golden brown.

Course, by the time her people had brought her back up here and dispersed her again, the meat wasn't safe for eating, Henrikson continued.

They don't salt them when they chop them up.

The vultures don't mind much.

Her mother and father, however, were as fresh as could be, brought up here just before sunset, I reckon. The birds had barely started on the eyes, which they're welcome to as I don't much care for them.

The agent looked at the ground. He kicked at the dirt. Kicked up the bones. Femurs, ribs, a jaw . . . Saw that what he had thought was a small rock that resembled a skull *was* a skull submerged in the sand. He felt a sharp pain in his stomach and winced. The bounty hunters noticed.

That'll be that rattler juice again, said Thrush. Not my cooking. None of us are cramping up. He looked round the others to verify.

That's right, said Henrikson. I've not had the shits from your cooking since . . . Whelp, I can't rightly say. Been a time, certainly.

And it's not from the meat, said Death Mask. I'm just saying. It all tastes the same.

Bet you thought he was talking about sucking dick?

Why would he think that? I don't have any lips to suck a dick with.

He could shoot them and take one of their horses. Was he fast enough to take out three bounty hunters before one of them stuck him . . ?

He retched, spat bile, but nothing substantial came up. His body was well on its way to digesting what he had eaten. Nothing he could do about that.

When he stopped heaving and spitting and looked up, the three men had their guns on him. They were calm about it though. Henrikson hadn't even bothered to stand.

Relax, old man. It's not like we killed them, said Thrush.

He killed them, said Death Mask. Remember?

That's right.

All we did was cook them up a little and eat them. Ain't nothing wrong with that.

We don't cook the ones we kill.

We sure do.

Because that would be wrong.

You did just the other day.

Shush. I was trying to be reassuring.

You know, said Henrikson, for a detective you're not particularly observant. This here is a burial site.

Good eating too, said Thrush.

It was only then that the drunken thoughts that had been troubling the agent during the night coalesced. The man had not killed the girl, was not dismembering her to hide what he had done. He was returning her to the earth. The agent had never seen it before but he had read about it. And it was unlikely the girl's father would have done such a thing if he was the one who killed her.

Though it was not out of the question.

People have done things more peculiar back in civilisation. The things they got up to out here you could not even comprehend.

That man you killed? said Henrikson.

And ate, said Thrush.

His daughter'd gone missing weeks before. Every day he looked for her. Spent every penny he had on trying to find her. Even returned to work, despite his grief, just so he could keep paying the trackers. Eventually they found her, brought her back to him, rolled up in a blanket on the back of a horse. She must have escaped to have been found at all. But her injuries . . . All he could do was give her peace. Then you go and scoop her up in a pillowcase, kill her folks and leave her to rot in a tent. That, my friend, might be worse than anything we've done.

It's up there, that's for sure, said Thrush.

Death Mask had cut two slits in a black bandana that he wore over his face. From the way he sat on his horse he did not look pleased about sharing it with Thrush. However, Thrush did not seem to mind, sitting with his crotch pressed against the rear of his companion, shuffling forward in the saddle every time Death Mask edged away, legs wrapped around the horse's neck.

I can't help it, he said. It's the vibrations what are doing it.

Thrush talked relentlessly but it could not truthfully be said that the group spoke much. Now and then one of them would ask the agent something and he would give them an answer—where he was from (Scotland), did he have a wife (Dead. That's right, you said that already.), kids (none (not strictly true)), how come he ended up being an agent (long story) . . . Now and then he would ask one of them something, if only because he did not like them knowing more about him than he did about them. Henrikson's answers were as non-committal and vaguely truthful as the agent's but Thrush was always happy to break the silence. Seemed Thrush never had a thought he never said aloud.

There used to be three of them.

Then Sally slipped on a goddamned overgrown bellybutton and couldn't walk and we had to drag him round the bottom of this frozen lake by his insides and hang him from a tree to escape from wolves, Thrush had said unprompted.

Sometimes I wonder, said Henrikson, when Thrush isn't speaking, does he think at all?

Mostly they hunted runaways.

A little scalp-hunting here and there.

Until they found out we'd just been going across the border and taking them from Mexicans.

There's still three of you now.

The agent tilted his head towards Death Mask.

Thrush turned around in his seat. They had swapped places on the horse. Thrush rode up front.

He, rather fortuitously, turned up just after Sally's position became vacant. Even had a bounty with him.

Two, said Death Mask.

That's right, Thrush said proudly. And the second one wasn't even on the manifest.

Thrush lowered his voice and spoke behind his hand.

Don't tell anyone but we never collected the bounty on that one.

Death Mask shook his head. Grinned.

You didn't eat it?

Oh heck no. Of course not. No. We sold her. And the baby.

Had it nice for a time, said Death Mask.

Until the money ran out.

Then it was back to work, tracking runaways and taking scalps and the like.

You said you were retired, said Thrush, turning the subject of the conversation back to the agent.

More or less. Winding down's what they call it. Next time I check in will be my last, said the agent.

Then what are you going to do?

Keel over and die, most likely.

What brings you out here anyway? asked Henrikson.

Missing kids.

This made Henrikson laugh longer than the agent would have preferred but he didn't ask what was so funny.

A GIRL HAD GONE MISSING, a year or so ago, give or take. Most likely she had wandered off and fell or got hurt somehow, bitten by a rattler, taken by wolves, that was the thinking. Well that's what folk said out loud but there were other thoughts too, that she'd been taken, ideas involving murder and sometime sex, which folk mostly kept to themselves or said only in hushed whispers.

The agent reported it, went out with one of the search parties, but otherwise did not investigate. The frontier is a dangerous place. More than likely the girl would have died during the winter in any case, even if she had not gone missing. Her parents did.

Then, some time after all this, he came to a reservation, discovered a girl had gone missing there too. He asked around to see if he could dig anything up, if you pardon the phrase. People tended to have a lot to say about the folks who lived on the reservation but they had nothing to say about the girl. They were preoccupied with the train that had been held up a couple of nights back. Nobody was killed. They seemed disappointed by that. They perked up at the news of the missing girl and took to calling her the dead girl even though she might not have been that way yet.

But she didn't turn up either.

The agent hung around to see if anything would arise, followed up a couple things on the train robbery and sent off a couple of telegrams to the office keeping them informed but the carnival arrived the second night he was there and that was the end of it. He saw a moving picture show, screamed along with everybody else at the train they thought was going to crash through the sheet on which it was shown, even though he had seen it before back east. He left the next morning, following the train line out of town until he came to a junction. One way was closed off by a sign that said Under Construction. He took that one.

On the way into the railroad camp he saw the pictures nailed to trees of more missing children. Not all girls. The women and men alike eyed him with suspicion, glowering from bloodshot eyes dried out from weeping. He did not stay long. Took down the basic details and moved on, riding through the night, not wanting to lie down until he was far from the camp. He was not sure what he was afraid of more: whatever it was that took the children or the families that thought it might have been him.

The stories were always the same: missing children; train robberies. Not always at the same time. Not all children went missing from towns or camps along the railroad, and the robberies did not always occur near to where a child had gone missing. There was no pattern.

He stopped pursuing the missing children. He had nothing to go on as none of them ever turned up. Not a body or even a bit of clothing. Any instances of missing kids he came across as he tracked the train bandits across the country he would write down what happened in his notebook and record the location on his map but it had thus far come to nothing.

The train bandits had been developing quite the reputation. Sketches of their leader appeared in stations, banks and post offices. The features were always slightly different—some sort of hat, bandana, stubble, no stubble. The only constant was the black eye. Some described it as being missing, others said it was a prosthesis, black as stone or coal, and some said that it was his actual eye, tattooed black. The rest of the details were slight. No name or age. Only what he was wanted for and the price on his head and the nickname he had acquired in the papers: Ghost Eye. And it was just such a poster that Henrikson pulled from his satchel, unfolded, and handed to the agent.

You know him? said Henrikson.

I'm familiar with the name, said the agent.

I thought you might be.

ghost eye seeker

FACE BLACKENED FROM THE FURNACE the fireman took his tin mug of coffee from the engineer with a barely perceptible acknowledgement, sipped and grimaced approvingly at the bitterness and leaned one arm out of the cab and drummed his fingers against the locomotive. Not quite a full moon but near enough, casting its red glow on the fresh stumps of felled trees by the side of the tracks and on the rails. With the engine hot and the mountain air cold the engineer and the fireman found themselves finally comfortable. Most of the passengers had taken to their bunks, huddling beneath blankets wearing everything they owned. Other than the blood-red tracks through the trees, the mountain was in darkness.

∞

Everywhere they found variations of the same theme: the remains of a train crumpled in a ravine beneath a bridge that wasn't there, passengers looking lost, insurance men, detectives and bounty hunters perusing the scene, and in the towns and camps and reservations nearby, whispers of a kid gone missing. They moved on. Henrikson was unfazed.

We'll get them eventually. No need to hurry.

∞

When they passed the only building they had seen for days they were shot at. They heard the bullets hit the dirt behind them before they heard the shots and they saw the barrel of a rifle briefly in a window before it disappeared leaving a waft of smoke behind.

Thrush and Death Mask dismounted. Their guns were holstered. They entered through the front door and did not come out again for a while. The agent went to follow but Henrikson held his arm and said to give them a minute. They came out empty handed, same as they went in, and mounted their horse. Thrush wiped his hands on his trousers and took the reins.

A man staggered out the small house, missing the top of his head. They did not see him. By the time anybody else came that way he would be buried in the dirt. The others in the house they would find and blame on the natives.

∞

The engineer looked at his watch. Theirs was not the

first locomotive through the passage but so far was the only one with paying passengers.

The fireman was looking at him over the rim of his mug.

Should be at the next incline in a minute or so, the engineer said.

The firemen went to put down his coffee but the engineer said, I'll get it, and shoveled coal from the tender into the fire.

The fireman finished his coffee and took the shovel off the engineer.

The engineer checked his watch again.

The fireman shoveled coal into the fire.

The engineer let more steam into the pipe. They were gaining speed. He tapped the fireman on the shoulder.

The fireman stopped shoveling.

Boss?

The engineer checked his watch. Then leaned out the cab.

Something wrong, boss?

The engineer took out a notebook from the pocket of his overalls and flicked through it. He checked his watch again, leaned out the cab again.

They were gaining speed. The engineer looked up, around. The trees had closed in on them. The peak of the mountain that had loomed over them was gone, out of sight.

The engineer laughed and shook his head.

Everything okay, boss?

For a moment there I thought we'd taken a wrong turn.

Why that's impossible. There hasn't been a junction in days.

It's these trees is all. We're making such good time and you're tending to that fire so fastidiously that for a while there I thought we were going downhill.

The fireman looked around at the trees, the tops of them visible, tinged red against the back sky, but the rest of them were in darkness.

Must not have cut these ones back, he said.

Wonder why.

Probably ran out of time.

Sure is hard to tell, isn't it, which way we're pointing. Like one of those electric roads. You heard of those?

It rings a bell.

They're some kind of optical allusion.

∞

Outside the sheriff's cabin there was a poster of Ghost Eye. The bounty was higher than on the one the agent had folded up in his satchel. Next to it was a smaller one, no picture, just words, hand-written slowly in different sized letters, most of them spelled correctly, about a missing girl. Another one. The ink was fresh but had bled. Outside the tavern was a tattered poster for a carnival, advertising a moving picture show and a special guest, Obediah Crow, the Mountain Man. The outline of their tents, leaflets and ticket stubs trampled into dirt, the smell of rotting popcorn and corndogs lingering.

∞

They never came into my cage. They would throw me scraps to eat, bowls of mush, thin stews, sometimes the scrag ends of meat I assumed were from other men. I never touched any of it.

At first.

I needed to build my strength up if I was to escape. They killed another man in front of me. Dismantled him, made pink soup and served it to me in a clay bowl, laughing, waiting for me to kick it over or throw it at them again. But I didn't. The man was dead. I'd been around these folks—if you could call them folks—long enough to see the respect they had for what they killed and what they ate.

White folk excepted.

I lifted the bowl to my lips. It smelled of iron, of blood, rust, like eating blood pudding with a burst lip. I supped it but it was too thick. So I gulped it down, gagging, trying not to think about what it was I was drinking. Eating.

Here's a question for you folks out there in the audience: does one drink soup or eat soup?

> *Drink soup.*
> *Bullshit—it's not a beverage.*

It's a liquid, is it not?

> *It can be.*
> *You eat soup.*
> *That's right. You drink broth.*
> *Bullshit, I say!*

Settle down folks. I was only jesting.

But you want to know something? If I'm being truthful, other than the fact that I was eating the brains and whatever else of another white man, you want to know something?

What?

If I'm being completely honest?

What?

Now this is something I've never told anybody else—

What is it, Obediah?

Well?

You know what? If I was being completely honest, I'd tell you that the soup was actually pretty damn good. Say what you like about those folk out there in the desert but they sure as all hell can cook. I ate their corn mush, their breads, their soup, the dried meat they tossed through the bars of my cage.

Then I realised they were fattening me up. It was getting cold. The weather was changing. The mountains, which I couldn't see before from the heat haze of the desert, had snow on them. They were going to fatten me up and take me with them when they moved on. I was to be a walking supply of meat.

Well, do you know what? Let them fatten me up? If I was going to survive out there in the desert in winter, then I was going to need as much meat on my bones as possible.

And they'd given me an idea.

∞

Without noticing when it happened, the agent realised they were riding through a flat expanse of sand. The mountains were gone. He looked behind but could not see where they had come from. In all directions the white stretched out to where it met the red sky, the horizon a smear of grease on glass. Eventually the sand gave way to cracked white earth and the horses' hooves crunched with each step. They stopped to let them chew on the dried black stringy leaves and bulbous pearls of the plants that grew in this desert.

You reckon there's enough water in them to keep the horses going?

It's that or whiskey.

Death Mask uncorked a bottle. Beads of sweat ran down his face that he continually wiped away with a bandana. He passed the bottle to Henrikson.

Too much of this and we're likely to burst into flames.

A plume of dust appeared on the horizon.

What's that? A dust devil?

It ripped a line in the dirt behind it, red dirt rising like smoke.

It's coming straight for us.

That's no dust devil.

Death Mask lifted his rifle and aimed with both eyes open.

He cocked the hammer, tracking the plume of dirt with the barrel.

They could hear it, the sounds of hooves on the desert floor.

Death Mask pulled the trigger and they saw the horse tumble out from the cloud of dirt, the rider thrown from the saddle.

The rider twitched on the hard earth. His limbs jutting out at unnatural angles. His eyeballs vibrated in his skull.

Ah shit, you got the horse, said Thrush.

Death Mask kicked through the letters that had spilled from the rider's post bag.

See if there's money in those, said Henrikson.

That's illegal, said the agent. Stealing people's mail.

He was coming right for us.

∞

They saw it for most of the morning, not getting any closer until, all at once, they were upon it, the lighthouse. The top was missing, the spiral staircase continuing beyond till it ended in a tangle of twisted iron. A ship on its side against the rocks, hull caved in. On what was left of the tower were holes the size of cannonballs.

But cannonballs could not have done this.

They rode around the carcass of the ship. Through a hole near the base of the lighthouse tower the agent found himself looking straight through to the other side.

Looks like it's been pierced right through.

Death Mask went to look in the dirt for the projectile. The agent and Thrush looked inside. Henrikson remained on his horse.

The lighthouse was empty, ransacked some time before. They found a bottle of rum inside the ship, saw the empty shackles of cargo in the hold but that was it.

Look what I got, boss, said Thrush, holding up the bottle of rum for him to see the dark liquid sloshing inside like oil.

Oh good, said Henrikson. If the whiskey doesn't cause us to combust then a bottle of gunpowder between us should see to it easily.

∞

When the agent returned to his horse it lay down on the ground and died. Thrush was not pleased.

That's the last time I loan you anything, he said.

They butchered the horse and lit a fire and ate a little bit. The rest they packed away.

Horses don't eat meat, do they? asked Thrush, trying to force a chunk of meat into his horse's mouth.

They don't eat horse, said Death Mask. They don't eat each other.

They spent the night outside the lighthouse. They debated what had happened to it for a time but soon lost interest. They weren't going to talk each other into finding out the right answer.

The next morning when they brushed the sand from their clothes they saw that it was not sand at all but the broken shells of crustaceans. The agent swept some sand away with his boot and took a closer look at the ground. He soon found some small ones that were intact, the creatures long gone. He held up a mollusk about an inch long and Thrush went over to have a look. Henrikson seemed to be aware of it already, or at least acted like he was, whilst Death Mask ignored it, kept his face hidden in his hood from the black hole in the sky.

∞

The engineer lit his pipe and rested his back against the door of the cab, every now and then leaning over to look ahead onto the tracks.

It certainly feels like we are increasing in speed.

The engineer took a long draw on his pipe, checked his watch again.

Any of that coffee left?

The fireman felt the weight of the coffee pot, shook it.

Little bit.

He poured some into the engineer's mug. The engineer sat it on the floor of the cab and crouched to look inside it.

The fireman let a sigh escape from his nostrils.

Something wrong?

Bring that light over.

The fireman lifted the lantern off its hook and squatted over the tin mug.

Do you see something?

Does that coffee look flat to you?

The fireman angled his head one way, then the other.

Nope. Can't say this is the smoothest track we've

ever taken.

Not still. Flat. Level.

Hard to say with all the bumping. Why'd you ask?

Looks to me like there's less distance between the coffee and the rim of the mug at the front than there is at the back.

Meaning what? said the fireman, pretending he was following where this was going.

In other words, this mug is at angle. This whole train is at an angle. You were right. We are going faster. Because we are going downhill.

The engineer stood and turned the handle to close off the steam pipe. He leaned out the cab.

We must have gone over the top already, said the fireman.

The engineer checked his watch.

Maybe, he said.

But he did not think so. Not yet.

He put a hand on the brake, still leaning out the side of the cab.

We're making good time is all, said the Fireman, hopefully, proud of his shoveling skills, even if they had led to this momentary period of uncertainty. He leaned out the other side of the cab, felt the wind rushing past, felt it cool his heat-tightened skin.

∞

More sand, broken shells, upturned boats, and dried seaweed to chew on. Another horse dead.

Doesn't matter, said Death Mask. None of them'd make it across.

Even Henrikson dismounted and walked with them.

They could feel the heat of the desert floor beneath the soles of their boots. The remaining horse began to moan. Its hooves were melting, strings of adhesive clinging to each one. Its feet soon became stuck and its legs buckled beneath it.

Ain't you going to shoot it, said the agent.

Can't spare the bullet, said Henrikson.

All around were the dried-out husks of other animals who had tried to make it, urged onwards by their riders. The further they got, the less there were.

They came to a little domed building, roof like a turtle shell and a tunnel-entrance to crawl into. Expected it to be baking inside but instead it was cool. Light shone through the cracks in the sand-bricks it was made from. There was some bedding on the floor.

Bet it gets cold out here at night, said Thrush. You'd want someone to snuggle up next to.

Death Mask squirmed. Thrush saw the agent looking at him. He nodded towards the bedding.

Count them, he said.

There were three.

A family?

The agent crawled outside, shielded his eyes from the sun. Still nothing in any direction. His eyes hurt. If he had any fluid in his body to spare, his eyes might have watered, but all he had was whisky and whatever he could squeeze out the boils of the black weed. Even with his hand shielding his eyes he had to screw up his face.

I don't know how he manages, he muttered.

There was no way Death Mash could see anything at all. And yet the agent had seen him shoot. Did not necessarily like what he shot, or who, but he could admire a good marksman when he saw one. Particularly if that person was blind, say.

This dwelling was occupied and the agent did not want to be there when whoever was occupying it returned. Not if Death Mask and Thrush and Henrikson were there when they did.

I'm going to ride on, he told them, even though he had nothing to ride on. I've got ants in my pants.

Henrikson nodded. Death Mask stared. Thrush rubbed his hands together.

∞

Three of them. Wrapped in furs as though the white dust they walked on was snow. A man and two women. Either could have been his wife or his daughter. A son, even. He waved to them and they waved back.

One of the women opened a drawstring bag and showed him what was inside, took a handful and offered it. It was black, dried. She poured it into his hand. He sniffed it, smelled the smoke.

Tea? he asked. He mimed drinking. Tobacco?

Still she just looked at him.

To smoke, he said.

She shook her head and smiled. She took a piece out of his hand. Its colours changed from dark to purple to green as she put it in her mouth.

Is that pyototo or whatever you call it? I can't be doing with one of those mind-altering experiences. Real-life out here is bad enough, I got to spend more time exploring my own skull? No thank you, ma'am.

She laughed and pointed at the ground. At the seaweed. Mimed picking the weed, putting some in her mouth.

She offered it to him again and he tried it. It was salty, smoky. Best thing he'd had since . . . he could not remember.

She had him open his satchel and poured a couple handfuls into it. All he had to offer her was a little of the rum in his water flask but he didn't want her to burst into flames. Then he remembered the poster of the Mountain Man Obediah Crow. He took it out and unfolded it and handed it to her. When she saw the image she shook her head and backed away. She looked at her father or her husband and her mother or her sister and they spoke quickly among themselves and shook their heads and started moving.

Hey, where you going?

He ran after them.

Don't go that way, he tried to get in front of them but they were too fast, even in their heavy furs. Don't go, he croaked.

He pulled out his gun and fired into the air. They turned and saw him with his badge and his gun and they turned and huddled over, shuffled onwards.

Shit, he said. Shit shit shit.

Then later: Fuck.

He heard the ringing of gunshots soon after. Felt a little of himself leaving. He did not stop. Closed his eyes.

When he opened them again it was dark and before him the land glowed with burning orange rivers and streams flowing in the sand. Fire on the mountains. He heard voices, curses, singing, swearing, the clanging of metal on metal, the thwack of metal on wood, wood on flesh, of leather on skin—

∞

The red moon had returned. The trees, though still dense, had thinned a little. Paths and trails wound through them.

The engineer let his shoulders and his chest loosen up. He kept his hand on the brake. The fireman's head jerked around like he had seen something.

What?

A light. Must've been a campfire or a cabin or something.

Out here?

Out everywhere. But they'll up sticks soon enough, now that the railroad has caught up with them.

They can only go so far. Soon it'll have crossed the country in every direction.

Some folks just aren't for settling. Some folks,

society has not served them well.

The engineer, who had been served soundly by society, could not disagree. He took his hand off the brake. Paths and trails meant there were animals and, at this speed, a cowcatcher did nothing but push the poor creature till it tore apart. Best to hit them fast and vaporise them, else he would have to watch some elk or bear get torn into bits, caught in the machinery, and then he would have to stop and untangle the bloody mess.

Looks like they've started moving already, said the fireman.

Pardon me? said the engineer, who had been alone in his thoughts.

First sight of the train and they've up and left.

You jest.

The fireman pointed behind the engineer at the blinking lights moving through the trees. The engineer turned and saw them for himself. A trail of torches snaking between the black limbs.

Pioneers, said the fireman. Got to admire them.

Scoundrels.

The engineer put his hand back on the brake. The lights were closer, casting shadows of twisting branches on the track.

That's rather a lot to be moving this time of night, the fireman muttered. You don't think—

The engineer looked over.

Indians?

The lack of panic in the fireman's voice suggested he

did not believe this to be the case but nobody likely believed it to be the case until the top of their head was hanging by its hair from a belt.

The engineer let go of the brake and released more steam into the pipe.

Best we don't stop then. Just in case.

The fireman picked up the spade and started shoveling coal into the furnace and did not stop until the lights had disappeared into the trees behind them.

∞

When the sun rose again there were no mountains. The red sand turned black, like it was covered in soot or ash—the sky had grown darker and he could still smell fire—but it was the sand that had burned, in some places turned to glass. He could hear it tinkle as it rushed to fill the indentations of his footprints and crack beneath his weight. Half-buried in the black sand was the cogged wheel of a machine. White against the black landscape. He ran his hand across it dusting away the sand, rubbing it into the grooves of the raw wood. The further he ventured, the more he saw: wooden wheels, panels, pipes, machinery, chimneys, boilers, cowcatchers, tools, spades, hammers, rods, and all the parts that make up a locomotive laid out on the sand like assembly instructions in a catalogue. His path wound through the stumps of trees cut down to make them.

∞

The sky was dark but night was yet to fall. Rivers of burning fire ran in channels through the sand. He heard voices barking orders, swearing, laughing, grunting, the occasional howl of pain . . . He saw the same shapes—the cogs, the wheels—emerge from the black earth as liquid fire filled their negatives, saw the barefoot boys without shirts digging channels for the molten gold to run, saw cauldrons of the stuff boiling over fires tended to by square men with arms like country hams, carpenters shaping and sawing the wood, and more boys laying the wooden shapes in the sand, their imprints to be filled with lava—

Out the fuckin way ya bam, one of the boys shouted. He wore the same flat cap as the rest of them.

What ye daein ya fuckin tube? said another.

One of the men jerked a meaty thumb over his shoulder.

The agent held up both hands in apology. He stumbled but kept his balance.

Sake man, shouted the boy at his feet whilst the other lobbed a shovelful of sand at him. He blinked and looked down. He had stood in the boy's work, ruined the wheel he had just prepared.

Sorry, he said. Sorry, sorry, he repeated, making his way through the men.

When he got to the entrance, he asked a man where he was.

This is the desert, son, said the man. He was several years younger than the agent.

Behind the man a sign said IRONWORKS. He could

not make out the word above it.

Where's that? he asked, gesturing towards the rows of lights from buildings further down the hillside.

That's the town.

The agent considered showing the man his badge but he didn't. He really could not be bothered.

∞

He was greeted by the usual wanted posters, Ghost Eye among them—*I heard he commandeered a ship and ate the crew; I heard he sold his family into slavery: I heard he was a slave; I heard he sold his whole village; Told them they were goin to America but threw them overboard; And they were eaten by sharks*—and another missing child. The ink was fresh on both posters. The bounty was high but had not been scored out and replaced with a bigger one. It was new. He was close.

Rows of houses filled with hard bastards and their harder wives and ugly offspring. Through the single uncurtained window of one he saw a box bed, pull-out drawers below that for the children to sleep in, a fire and stove opposite. At the end of the row was the wash house.

He knocked on the door and cleared his throat. Several women looked up from their washing. Threads of hair clung to their foreheads. Veins in their forearms throbbed.

Aye, said one of them, her hands up to her elbows in the tub, scrubbing denim on a washboard. That's the stitchin on the crotch gone again. For a man wi a wee willy he doesnae half go through the crotch.

Maybe his wee willy's pokin holes in it?

Excuse me, said the agent again.

Aye?

He took off his hat, rotated it between his thumbs.

I was wondering if you might be able to tell me—

Aye?

—where I might find a hotel or a saloon?

Aye. Main Street. Up there, she jerked her head, still scrubbing. Turn right. That's Main Street.

You'll know it's Main Street because it's the main street, said her companion at the mangle.

Big hoose that says HOTEL ootside. That's you.

She looked back down at the washboard, cleaning the denim like she was drowning a pig.

∞

Together they stood, looking back at the carriages, the engineer still clutching the handle of the steam pipe. He turned it slowly. They both laughed but it was a laugh that was more like an exhalation, like they had been holding the air in for some time. They smiled. Looked at the floor. Shook their heads.

Probably pioneers.

Hunters.

Mountain folk.

I hope not.

Indians wouldn't use lanterns.

Not if they were planning on ambushing the train.

I've never heard of Indians ambushing a train.

The fuck, shouted the engineer, not normally one for profanities, shutting the steam pipe and reaching for the brake.

The fireman leaned out the cab.

The track, it's—

He alternated between turning the handle for the steam pipe and pumping the brake. The train shuddered and jolted and they could hear the startled yelps and screams of the passengers in their bunks in the carriages behind them, even over the roar of the fire and the water bubbling and sloshing in the boiler and the steam vents whistling and the brakes hissing and the wheels screeching and rattling on the rails—

—gone.

The tracks disappeared and the locomotive careered down the hillside, sand spraying up the sides like the wake from a ship, hurtling through trees, the engineer trying frantically to keep the vessel from capsizing. The fireman held onto the cab door, watching the sand, stones, dirt and other debris torn up by the locomotive being thrown into the air and scattered beside them.

∞

They were waiting for him at the bar. Thrush patted the seat next to his. The agent took it, nestled between Thrush and Henrikson. Death Mask sat on the other side of Thrush. His eyes burned red even in the gloom.

Henrikson supped a whisky. All three had their hats on. Other than a young woman trembling by the piano, the place was empty. On the wall behind her was a poster advertising Obediah Crow. Thrush saw the agent looking.

You ever seen him before?

One time. I believe you were also there.

That's right.

Why do they call you Thrush anyway? I assume it's not your real name.

It could be my real name.

Is it though?

Naw. It's because I like birds.

It's because you're an irritating cunt, said Henrikson. Get the man a drink.

Death Mask reached behind the bar and lifted a bottle of something brown and viscous. He poured a glass full of it and slid it towards the agent but it got stuck on the bartop and the brown liquid sloshed over the edge of the glass.

Parched, the agent downed it in one. He stifled a cough.

Not bad, is it? said Death Mask.

The agent hiccupped.

Henrikson finally looked at him.

What took you so long? he said.

∞

When they came to a stop the cab was on its side. The

engineer and fireman were bruised, scraped and shaken but otherwise okay. The locomotive was partially buried in the dirt, its nose completely hidden. They looked up at the mountain, saw their path through the trees, which were bent and broken like splintered pencils. The train had gouged a black scar out of the hillside. All but the first few carriages were upright.

The fireman slapped the engineer on the back, shook his head as if to say, You're one lucky bastard, but instead said, That's some driving son, and told him that he would buy him a drink some day, wondering when that day might be, given that they were still halfway up or down a mountain without anybody knowing for three days, when they didn't arrive at the next stop, that something was wrong.

The passengers of the upright carriages started to clamber out of them. Most stood gawping at the damage done, shaking their heads in disbelief, covering their mouths with trembling fingers, shaking hands, hugging one another, laughing, happy to have survived, whilst a few others went to check on the state of those still in the carriages that were on their sides. Something distracted them, made them turn towards the trees and point at the lanterns and the men and women who carried them, made them say things like, *Oh thank goodness* and *Help has arrived*, but it had not.

∞

Death Mask went away for a few days, said he was

going to follow up on some rumours regarding Ghost Eye's whereabouts. The agent caught a little of Obediah Crow's show but couldn't stomach it and went upstairs early.

∞

First they bound his wrists together and hoisted him into the air. Then two men took to slicing off his skin, starting with the soles of his feet. They worked quickly so my companion wouldn't die before they had finished. When they got to his knees they used their knives to undo the joints and his legs dropped to the dirt like two sticks. Then they worked their way up to his groin, peeling off the skin and muscle of his thighs and unfastening the bones at the sockets so the thigh bones dropped and rung out like a glockenspiel when they hit the other bones. Then they took to his stomach, his chest, peeling and filleting, the man, my companion, hollering the whole time. Soon all that hung from the post was two skinned arms, a screaming face without ears or lips or eyelids or teeth, and the raw meat of his body, ending at his genitals. Then they stopped. This last bit they had to do quickly but meticulously. Almost in one movement they sliced off his cock and his balls and opened his stomach with a knife and swung an axe into his chest so that just seconds after his guts unravelled onto the floor like a wet coil of rope his ribcage sprung open and you could see with your own eyes my companion's lungs when he took his last breath and his heart as it squeezed its last couple of drops that seeped from his whole body and he died.

That's when I decided to leave.

∞

Even from his bed he could hear Thrush laughing loudly. The carnival had already left. Obediah Crow was gone by morning. Thrush and Henrikson spent their time in the bar, drinking it dry.

Another girl's gone missing, said Death Mask, taking a seat beside them and pouring himself a whisky.

Ghost Eye, said Thrush.

How far? said Henrikson.

About half a day. I must have rode past them. I only found out about it on my way back.

When did this happen?

Two or three days ago?

Shit, said Thrush.

Alright, said Henrikson. Let's go. He got down off the stool, the first time the agent had seen him do so since they arrived. He was completely steady on his feet, no sign of the best part of four days drinking.

They left without paying. Nobody said anything, never even looked out of their doorways to watch the four strangers depart. They knew the strangers had gone after Ghost Eye. They were proud to have had them stay a while, the men who would capture and maybe even kill Ghost Eye, robber of trains, killer of wolves—

I heard he took the eye from the body of a shaman.

I heard he can still see through his missing eye. That it was taken by a bird and it sees everything.

Like a god.

I heard he is a god.

I heard he was an Indian.

An Indian god.

A shaman.

One of those ones that fucks and eats corpses.

I heard that Ghost Eye's a woman.

They all laugh.

I heard he's a one-eye, but he had a doctor cut his face up to make it look like he has two . . .

cruelty & waste

An eye opens. The gentle rustling of dry earth. The creak of leather rubbing against itself. The cracking and popping of joints and the barely perceptible nostril-wheeze of a shadowed figure straining to haul itself out of the earth. The groan of floorboards flexing beneath the boots of an intruder. The squeak of the hinges of the front door suggesting more than one. Further groaning, creaking, then the crash of a pan or something like it hitting the floor and the hushed voice of a man swearing and another whispered voice not apologising. The blackened figure creeps silently on hands and feet towards the cabin and lets itself in through the side door, skulks in the shadows and waits. Sees them through the open doorway searching the bedroom. The empty closet, beneath the bed, behind the door. Sees the pistols hanging from their belts, rifles in hands, useless indoors. A third man crosses the hallway. Sawn-off shotgun. Sensible. She snips his backbone with a hunting knife through his coat and takes the shotgun from him and has opened up the two prowlers in the bedroom before the man crumples like a discarded marionette, eye quivering in his useless slack face drooling. She searches his pockets and loads the shotgun with the shells she finds and empties the gun, empties his head. There are an infinite number of combinations a human head can take following a shotgun blast, including that of a perfectly formed human head. His does not recombine in such a way.

A HORDE OF WOMEN AND ONE-EYES, outcasts, misanthropes, murderers and molesters and convicts and slaves and other primitives came from out of the trees. Some entered the rear carriages of the train, the others surrounded it. They tore open valises and cases, tossed jackets and mattresses. The women got the passengers to empty their pockets and hand over purses without taking their guns from their holsters. A group of children in rags huddled together and when one of the gang went to make them open their meagre packs, Ghost-Eye whistled and they left them alone. Everything was emptied in a pile and counted and sorted by another one-eye, his long fingers lifting out strings of jewellery beads and laying them gently beside the others. Another lot manhandled the safe from the post car outside and set to opening it. The belongings and coins taken from the passengers were sorted into piles of similar worth and redistributed amongst the passengers. A man in a clean jacket and hat protested and earned a punch to the temple.

The bounty hunters and the agent looked at first to be with the gang, arriving on their horses, guns drawn. Then one of the passengers saw that the agent had his badge in the air and was hollering something but nobody could hear him over the screams and the gunfire and the groans of heavy metal and stone.

Henrikson picked off a few of the train robbers with his pistol, closing one eye and taking aiming down the barrel, as if only to show that he could. Thrush and Death Mask picked off some more. The train robbers took cover and returned fire.

The agent took a shot to the leg and dropped from his horse. He dragged himself across the ground but hands grabbed his coat and turned him over. He laid his back against the rail, pressing down hard on the bubbling hole in his thigh.

Before him was the one he had been chasing. The one known as Ghost Eye.

Ghost Eye's face was hidden beneath the shadow of the brim of his hat.

Ghost Eye's mouth was covered by a black bandana.

Ghost Eye's eye reflected fire but it was not his real eye.

Ghost Eye was not as tall as the agent had imagined.

Ghost Eye held a gun in one hand as though feeling its weight, like he was weighing up the cost of the agent's life.

At his side were two one-eyes. One female; one male. They too had guns. None of them aware of the three bounty hunters creeping up behind them.

Thrush and Death Mask raised their weapons. The one-eyes crumpled like they had been dropped feet-first from a height. Henrikson put a bullet through Ghost Eye's hand before Ghost Eye had even cocked the hammer. The gun lay on the ground.

It was the last thing the agent saw before his head was a puff of pink mist. Thrush holstered his weapon.

They tied up Ghost Eye and dragged him bleeding behind a horse for a while. Then they stopped and loaded him onto the back of it. It started to rain.

The horses ploughed a path that slowly filled in behind them as they drew their hooves sucking from the red mud. Henrikson untied Ghost Eye and dropped her into the sludge.

Thrush took hold of the rope still tied around Ghost Eye and hauled her to her feet but her legs buckled so he settled for dragging her towards the jail. Faces appeared in windows and doorways and lanterns were lit and soon a small crowd had ventured into the rain and gathered around the jail where the bounty hunters waited for the sheriff to answer, the words *Ghost Eye, they've captured Ghost Eye* spreading like a virus through the swelling crowd.

They caught Ghost Eye?

Sure did.

No way.

Shit you not.

I heard he killed a hundred wolves.

I heard it was five hundred.

A hunting party came across it. Three hundred

wolves.

I heard he stole a train and drove it off a bridge.

I heard he leads a gang of one-eyes—

And to join you have to scoop out one of your eyes with a knife.

And if you don't, they kill you.

I heard he eats kids.

A sleepy looking young man opened the door of the jail, yawning and rubbing his eyes. He smelled of bourbon.

You the sheriff? Thrush asked.

Does it look like he's the sheriff? Henrikson sighed.

Once saw an eleven year old boy who was sheriff, mused Death Mask. Everyone else was dead.

That so?

Sure is. It was but a prelude to my own brief and uneventful period in law enforcement.

You were in law enforcement?

Sure was.

What did you do?

I was sheriff.

The sheriff's home, said the young man. I'm deputy. We have Ghost Eye.

I beg your pardon.

Christ. Ghost Eye. Outlaw, gang leader, fugitive, runaway, murderer, train robber, child killer . . .

Give me a minute, said the deputy and went back inside. He came out with a poster and his eyes went from the poster to the bounty and back again several times.

That's him! he said.

That's a her.

Ghost Eye's a girl?

She's got tits, don't she?

Hell, if that's all it takes, I guess that makes me a girl too.

It's Ghost Eye, said the deputy.

You want her or not? Henrikson was getting impatient.

Of course! Bring him—*her*—in.

The money first.

Money?

The bounty. We don't do this for free and I'm not planning on sticking around.

The deputy looked again at the poster.

Listen Mister . . .

Henrikson.

We don't have that kind of money. We'll have to have it wired.

We're not sticking around. You want the girl, you have to pay.

W-what if we can't?

What's the poster say? Dead or alive?

Uh-huh.

Then we'll kill her. Keep the head till we get somewhere that can pay us.

Aw jeez. I bet the sheriff would surely like to be the one who hanged Ghost Eye.

You best get him then. We'll wait.

The deputy returned shortly with the sheriff. Ghost

Eye blinked and swayed on her feet, trying to take them in. The sheriff was fully dressed, though it looked like he had done so in a hurry and in the dark. His badge was upside-down.

Go and wake Mister Klay, he said to the deputy. He scanned the many faces of the crowd. If he is not already alerted to the situation.

This him? said the sheriff to Henrikson.

This is Ghost Eye.

It's not a *him*, added Thrush. That—he kicked Ghost Eye in the back of the knee and she dropped to the mud—is a *her*.

But it's Ghost Eye alright, said Death Mask. See for yourself.

He lifted Ghost Eye's head out the mud and pried open her eyelid to display the black stone behind it.

Well I never, said the sheriff, pushing up his hat, which was on backwards.

The deputy returned with the bank manager. He had a suit jacket on over his pyjamas. The sheriff explained the situation. The bank manager said, I see, I see a number of times, like he was about to provide a reason for why it might not be such a good idea to pay these bounty hunters using the money in the bank, *after all, it is not our money, it is theirs*, he would have whispered, signaling towards the crowd with an outstretched hand, but each time he tried to do so the sheriff cut him off.

The bounty hunters followed the sheriff and the deputy and Mister Klay to the bank, Thrush dragging Ghost Eye behind him. She did not attempt to stand.

The bank manager went inside. When he came out, he had a brown sack in his hand, which he gave to the sheriff. The sheriff peered inside.

It's all there, said Klay. I counted it twice.

The sheriff peered again, as though to confirm. He held it out to Henrikson. Henrikson nodded at Thrush, who handed the end of the rope to the deputy. The deputy took it like he had been asked to hold a dog turd.

The sheriff offered his hand to shake but Henrikson drew his pistol and shot Ghost Eye in the leg. The sheriff jumped back. The deputy dropped the rope and scrambled in the mud to pick it up again even though Ghost Eye was not going anywhere.

The sheriff put his hand on his gun but Henrikson shook his head.

What the hell did you do that for? he hollered, hand still on his gun.

The poster said dead or alive. Henrikson smirked.

But we paid you for alive, squealed the sheriff.

You best get to it then.

Ghost Eye bleeding out in the mud.

Shit, said the sheriff. Then, to the bank manager, he said, Get the damn doctor.

Henrikson turned and held up the sack of money.

Come on boys, he said to Thrush and Death Mask, who followed him. Let's go celebrate.

Henrikson stopped.

Hey, sheriff, he called out.

What? Damn you.

Mightn't you point us in the direction of the nearest drinking establishment?

Go to hell.

Henrikson laughed.

∞

Seemed the rest of the folk in town had the same idea and the celebrations soon spilled out into the street. Within the hour the road was knee-deep in vomit, the walls of taverns spattered with blood and loose teeth embedded in doors. The bounty hunters watched with delight from their stools at the bar. Although they were flush with money, drinks were on the house.

This town . . . said the bartender, a tear coming to his eye. When folks hear about Ghost Eye . . . when they heard that this is where they hanged him—

Her, someone corrected him. Ghost Eye is a her.

Like it matters.

The local newspaper had already sent their photographer to the jail to get a picture of Ghost Eye before she croaked.

There'll be a trial, said Death Mask happily.

Excuse me, said one of the many locals lurking at the bar, trying to get as close to the three bounty hunters as possible, so they could say later that they spoke with the men who caught Ghost Eye, had shaken their hands, bought them a drink . . .

You can't just hang a person without there being a trial first. It's the law.

That can't be right, said the man.

It is, said Henrikson, his lips around a bottle of beer.

The man shook his head.

Henrikson swallowed.

God-damn, he said. How long will that be?

A week, said Henrikson. Give or take.

A week?

Could be longer. Witnesses and so forth.

She's got the right to defend herself, said Death Mask.

Innocent until proven guilty, added Thrush.

God-damn, said the man again, louder, slamming his bottle of beer down hard on the bartop. Foam erupted from the neck, which he tried to sook before it ran down his hand. God-damn it.

That's the way it goes, said Henrikson, patting the man on the back.

The bartender had his arms crossed and he had been shaking his head for some time.

Motherfucker, he muttered. Mother-fucker. Mother. Fucker . . .

You all right there, big fella, said Henrikson.

Motherfucker.

Hey partner. You alright?

God-damn I'm not alright. Motherfucker's been robbing trains and fucking kids and we got to give him—*her*!—a chance to defend herself before she hangs? It's not right. It's not right I tell you.

What if, said the man at the bar, picking up the thread, what if she doesn't hang?

What do you mean?

What if she gets let off?

Why would she get let off? That's Ghost Eye, ain't it? Child-fucker . . .

Child-killer . . .

Cannibal . . .

Runaway . . .

Escaped convict . . .

I heard she plucked out her own eye and ate it . . .

Stranger things have happened, said Henrikson, taking another sip to hide his smile.

God-damn it.

We should kill her right now.

Sheriff's got a doctor working on her right now.

The sheriff's got a damn doctor working on Ghost Eye as we speak.

Motherfucker. The bartender smashed a bottle on the floor.

Didn't you see? Our man here shot her on the steps of the bank.

Henrikson touched the brim of his hat.

You're god-damn fucking kidding me.

How could you have missed it?

The bartender climbed onto the bar and whistled. Nobody paid him any attention. He whistled again, hollered for quiet a few times, but when that didn't work he settled for hurling a bottle at the piano. It smashed over the keys and showered the pianist in broken glass. The man stopped playing and the room fell silent.

Ladies and gentlemen, said the one-eyed pianist, picking shards of glass from his hands, I think your attention is wanted.

The bartender took a few deep breaths, tried to steady his anger, but couldn't and let it all come out in a rush, how the *motherfucking kid-fucking train-robbing cannibal Ghost Eye's in jail and a doctor is trying to save her fucking life so that said baby-eating Cyclops can stand trial and defend herself against the charges and might even go fucking free*—

We should kill her right now!

Let her hang!

Pull her fucking insides out and hang her by those!

One-eyed motherfucker!

Shots were fired and the pianist's head erupted and the piano keys tinkled as bits of it landed on them.

The three bounty hunters at the bar took this all in. They seemed pleased and stayed seated when the crowd piled into the streets.

Another drink gentlemen? Henrikson walked behind the bar and tossed a cloth over his shoulder.

THE ENTIRE TOWN, IT SEEMED, even without Henrikson's gentle provocation, had worked themselves up into the same frenzy and gathered around the entrance to the jail. The deputy was the first to come out. He did not say much, just took in the braying mass of angry men and women with a slack jaw and ashen face. He soon disappeared inside, closing the door behind him.

The sheriff's office was a single story stone building. Inside were two desks, one for the sheriff and one for the deputy. There was a little table and a couple extra chairs and a set of stairs that wound down through the dirt to the cells underground, where Ghost Eye was laid out on the floor being tended to by the doctor. The sheriff stood over them and looked up, exasperated, when the deputy came down the stairs in a hurry, struggling to say what he meant to say.

Out with it boy, instructed the sheriff.

It's . . . it's . . .

Well?

Take a deep breath, son, said the doctor, kindly.

The sheriff climbed onto a stone bed built into a cell wall and looked out between the bars of the small window below the ceiling, out onto the ground outside. When it rained, sludge from the street poured in through the bars, seeped down the wall into the bed, onto the floor. It was raining then. He wiped the mud from his hands on his trousers.

Shit, said the sheriff. Come with me.

The deputy followed him upstairs. The sheriff opened a cupboard and tossed a shotgun to the deputy and picked one out for himself. He put a box of shells on his desk, loaded the rifle and put a handful in his pocket. He drew his pistol and checked it. Then he holstered it.

You ready? he asked the deputy.

The deputy was not ready. But he had a shotgun in his hands and shells in his pocket.

Alright then.

He unlocked the door of the office and stepped outside to face the crowd.

What do you want? he yelled.

Give us Ghost Eye.

You can't have her.

Then we'll take her.

You'll have her soon enough.

Then why wait, sheriff?

What if she dies?

Then she dies.

She needs to be punished.

The doctor's taking care of that right now.

Let her die! someone called out.

Let us do it.

Let's hang her right now.

Nobody is hanging anyone tonight, said the sheriff. The doctor is patching up her wound. She's going to be fine. There will be a short trial, then she will be publicly hanged. You can all come and pay your respects then.

But nobody was listening and even if they were they would not have understood what he said beneath the sound of frothing blood bubbling up from his gullet. The deputy sat on the ground, back against the door, both hands limply cradling his gut. He was still alive when he was manhandled out of the way and tossed aside.

The door to the cells had been locked.

Get the damn keys, ordered the bartender.

Two men went to check the desks.

The bodies, he shouted. Check their pockets.

A few other people searched the pockets of the sheriff and the deputy, rolling their corpses over, coming up empty handed.

Check the floor. Maybe they fell out, shouted the bartender.

They dropped to their knees and sank their hands into the mud, feeling for the keys.

Shit. Ain't going to find anything in this.

Bullets didn't even put a dent in the cell door, but they did ruin the kneecap of the man who shot at it.

A door like that's going to need dynamite.

You got any?

The bartender, who had become the de facto leader of the mob, barged his way outside.

I can see them, somebody shouted.

He pushed through the crowd to the barred windows near the ground. He crouched and looked inside. The doctor was looking up at them. He held a rifle. Behind him, sitting upright on the bed of a cell, was Ghost Eye, looking worse for wear but alive. Her leg had been bandaged.

Best you let us have her, doc, said the bartender.

He saw the doctor's chest rise and fall.

I don't think I'll be able to do that, Earl.

That's not a wise decision, doc.

Why do you say that?

That there is a bad person. You should have let them die. Or better yet, let us have her.

Patching up bad folks is a bad decision? I best get a new profession then. He looked up at the bartender without blinking. He had patched up Earl more than once. Even sewn up his torn urethra and helped him with the story to tell his wife.

Tell you what, doc . . . You unlock that door and we'll let you go. If not . . . well . . .

You're going to kill the only doctor for a hundred miles?

If it comes to it.

That's not a wise decision, Earl.

Earl put both hands on his knee and pushed himself upright.

God-damn motherfucker, he said. Then: Dynamite it is. Get the god-damn explosives. Let's explode this fuckin bitch.

The dynamite was a long time coming from the mine. Didn't arrive until the morning. That was alright, they had time. Some folk went home, had breakfast or put on proper clothes, but most of them waited beneath oilskins, passing drinks to one another, sharing stories of the things Ghost Eye had done. By the time the horse came with the wagon of explosives the bounty hunters were gone, taking with them several bottles of whisky and whatever else they could carry from the tavern. Thrush wanted to take the girl who worked there but Henrikson said it was not a good idea, said if she fought the way she had during the night then she would only slow them down.

They wired up the dynamite and packed it around the door to the cells. The miners stood outside around the plunger, awaiting Earl's instructions. Even the gaffer had come with them when he found out what was happening. He held his tamping iron across his chest like a truncheon, tapping it against his open palm, waiting.

On Earl's command, the plunger was pushed and dynamite detonated. They expected some collateral damage to accompany the door being blown off but had not expected the whole building to implode, a cloud of red dust in the air followed shortly by trails of black smoke. Earl ran to the windows. Brick and stone and dust everywhere. The ceiling of the jail had collapsed.

Shit's on fire, he heard a voice say.

The fire soon engulfed the ruins. A silence set in among the crowd who gathered around, unsure of what to say. They seemed to have forgotten what it was they wanted, being so focused on each single event in turn—getting drunk, hanging Ghost Eye, getting into the cell, exploding the door—that it wasn't until somebody said *We did it!* that they realised that they had killed Ghost Eye, and the crowd cheered and the celebrations began again in earnest and the photographer snapped pictures of the destroyed jail house for the local paper.

∞

Inside, the doctor's body lay crushed beneath a broken beam. Ghost Eye remained on the bed, pinned in place by falling brick, watching helplessly as the fire spread towards her.

At first the fire hurt. Then it did not. This is it, she thought. Finally. She did not look at her body on fire.

She remained conscious, watching the black smoke above her head, hearing the rumbling of the fire and the restless stone changing shape and position.

∞

Ghost Eye, on fire, staggers blindly across the barren field . . .

∞

She was disappointed to have awoken on the back of another horse. She could not feel ropes or chains around her arms or legs this time. She could not feel anything. If not for the way her head flopped over the horse's flank she might as well have been just that: a head. Taken as a prize and tied up by her hair. The ground beneath her feet was a blur of rock and stone. The horse slowed and climbed carefully through wet clay, between boulders and broken wood, through skeletal trees. When they stopped she was lifted from the horse. She did not know by how many hands. Not many, for she was dropped onto the hard earth. She lay there for a time, waiting to die, until a wooden bowl was brought to her lips and the back of her head was lifted so she could drink from it.

∞

She was on her back. She looked over her body. Black mud had been spread thickly across her arms and legs and torso. She should have been cold.

You're awake, said a voice, high-pitched but earthy, like wind rustling through dead leaves.

The woman crouched down beside her and put the back of her hand on Ghost Eye's forehead. She could not see the woman's face beneath the twists of matted white hair, which the woman did not attempt to brush aside, but she felt familiar, like a family member not seen since childhood, vaguely recognisable. The woman was dressed in rags so caked in dirt and sticks they might as well have been made of the forest floor.

We can't stay here, the woman said. Take my hand.

Ghost Eye gripped the woman's hand with both of her own and the woman put her other hand on Ghost Eye's back and push-pulled her to her feet. She draped a dirty shawl around Ghost Eye and helped her onto the horse.

The mud will help cool the burns, she said. Try to get some sleep. We have a long way to go.

She gave her a piece of bark to chew.

This will help with the pain, she said, though Ghost Eye did not feel any. The woman took a piece for herself.

∞

It took several days. The woman only stopped to water and feed the horse. She would help Ghost Eye from the saddle and lay her on the ground. Then she would potter about like she was in a garden admiring her flowers and squat for a time before waking Ghost Eye and helping her up again.

This is us, said the woman when they came to the clearing. A wooden hut barely visible against the trees. A firepit. Scattered around the ground were bones of different sizes, different ages.

Don't worry, she said. They're not all human.

The woman lit a fire and led Ghost Eye towards it.

Get some sleep, she said. This won't be over quickly.

She cradled Ghost Eye's head in her arm and helped

her sup from the wooden bowl.

∞

Drifting in and out of consciousness she only glimpses what is done to her. A kettle bubbling over a fire, thick black smoke, the smell of medicinal herbs. Animal skins, hide, cut into strips and added to the liquor. She is given bark to chew on whenever the woman sees that she is awake. The same stuff that had been added to the pot. Needle and thread. Patches of blue-black leather. The scraping of cool wet mud from her limbs with a knife and the occasional lacerating pain of a live nerve being touched, at which the woman nods approvingly.

The woman laid the scraps of skin over Ghost Eye, cutting them to shape before she began. She held the needle up to the light. It took her a while to thread it.

When I said it won't be over quickly, this is why, she said, laughing, a sharp exhalation through the nostrils.

She gave Ghost Eye more medicine from the bowl.

When she woke the woman was gone. For several days she could not move. She lay there in the dirt beside the fire, watching it die. When the coals had gone gray and only a thin wisp of blue smoke remained, Ghost Eye could move her toes. Soon she could sit up, then stand. It took another few days of crawling before she could walk. Her skin squeaked and croaked when she moved. The leather would take a while to soften but the stitches held. Her new skin shone wet. She could not feel it but could sense the weight of it on her.

She touched her face, her head. Her sense of touch was gone but still she could not feel a difference between the skin of her head and that of her hands or the rest of her body, could not feel her fingers becoming tangled in her hair.

She looked around for the woman. She looked inside the cabin but did not stay there long. She did not want to catch herself in a mirror. She returned to her hole by the fire and buried herself in the dirt, willing herself to feel it cool against her dead new skin.

cyclops from the forge

More come to investigate but Ghost Eye is waiting for them. They follow the scrapings of her feet into the cabin but she is not inside. She crawls out from beneath it and locks the doors. Then she burns it down.

Others come to the fire. Ghost Eye sees their shadows flickering in and out as they dart between trees. It does not take them long to find what is responsible for the fire; it does not take Ghost Eye long to drag their bodies towards the it.

It is time.

THE BOOZE WAS LATE and there was an outbreak of good behaviour. The fronts of stores and houses were freshly painted and porches had been scrubbed clean of spat tobacco. Bruises had healed and scabs had fallen off and folk were discussing the books they were reading. Fingertips hardened from picking at the strings of instruments and people sat in threes playing guitars and banjos and fiddles and saws and jaw-harps and one of them would find a note under their breath and someone else would hear it and find it too and hum a little louder, one of them maybe attempting a harmony, muttering the words they remembered and humming where they lost them, wiping dust from the chrome buttons of an accordion, and a man with his hands in his pockets, tapping his feet, waiting for them to finish, whistling where it felt appropriate, the musicians smiling up at him, says, There's a pianer across at the saloon, if you want to take this down there I'll be sorely glad to accompany you and maybe we can earn us a little sarsaparilla each on the house, what do you say?

With shame they saw out the corners of their eyes the black square on the ground that was once the jail. They would look away, go quiet until they had passed it.

The teacher started turning up at school and parents remembered to send their children and they would come home able to write their names and count on their fingers, could think of what it was they wanted and could ask for it politely and for the first time the adults knew their kids were going to be alright, so instead of jumping down their throats when they picked up the fiddle they'd say things like *you're getting better* or *that's a tough one* or *here, let me show you something* . . .

The children got time off to help in the fields, to thresh the corn and the rye, to grind it into flour for bread or malt it for brewing, taking turns to clean out the mash tun or rolling barrels to the storeroom. Nobody knew to look for the spores on the grain. They cut it down and ground it up or malted it just the same.

An old-timer with an ear horn and a dirty union suit he had never been seen out of, worn with his gun and holster and a beat up old pair of boots and his bowler, said he could distil some that beer into whiskey, and some of the men went off to help build a still.

The cows were milked and the milk churned into butter and baked into cakes and the flour baked into bread and the musicians agreed upon a list of songs for the party and decorations were cut out of paper and coloured strips of cloth and sheets and lanterns slung from between the houses and posters were put up advertising the ceilidh even though everyone in town already knew about it and had a hand in making it happen.

And somebody who was passing through, a soldier on his way home, who had only stopped in for a drink and a screw but who'd been there five days already, sober and having the best sex he had ever had with a woman he knew had not been coerced in any way, said the last town he was in there was a travelling carnival, said there was this magic box that could make pictures move, said that on the wall there was this picture of a train and that the train was moving, *coming into station, coming right towards us and we thought it was going to come through the wall and run us down and we all screamed and tried to get out of the way and then laughed and helped each other up off the floor when of course the train didn't do any such thing*, said it would be wonderful if the carnival would come this way on the same night as the ceilidh, and everybody said that it was a truly wonderful idea and said they would get a messenger out to the carnival folk and the soldier himself volunteered, for he had taken a liken to this town, for one young woman in particular, and didn't see himself leaving anytime soon.

GHOST MAKES HER WAY on foot towards the coral glinting on the mountain range through the trees. There are some horses hitched at the edge of the forest, hungry and restless. She unties them but they stay where they are. She keeps away from the roads and mapped paths, staking new ground or following the desire trails of animals that disappear into cover and watch the black figure curiously from their hiding places. She crosses the desert of crushed crustaceans and climbs into the pink mountains, scrambling up the dead coral, the leather of her hands and knees tearing painlessly as she hauls herself up. The sun sets and rises several times and she does not stop. She does not look behind her. She reaches the top of the ridge and does not look out, keeps her eyes on her feet. She turns eastwards and makes her way towards the summit joining the switchback path that comes up from the other side. She does not take it to the summit. Instead she ventures carefully off the path to another, hidden by fallen stones and sand and brush, into a gully. She can hear it now, feel it, the rumbling beneath her feet, below the rocks, beneath the whistling of the wind. She is surprised at how steady she is on her feet given that she cannot feel them.

∞

There is a hole a little wider than a person hidden behind a bush of mesquite. She sits down on the lip of the hole with her legs dangling inside it. Then she drops down. Red dust disturbed by her appearance dances hesitantly in the air, settles on her new skin, on her lips, her tongue. The tunnel slopes downhill, as does the roof. If you were to sit still long enough you would see the rock flow and change shape. She follows the tunnel, crouching as the roof lowers, crawling on her knees, and finally working her way through on her stomach, turning her head to the side to fit through the lowest section, knowing that if she were to push against the stone unawares with her numb foot or elbow then she could bring it down upon her. And she knows it would not kill her. She would be trapped forever but she would not die. She pulls herself through to the other side.

∞

She is in a chamber the height of several men. Holes bored in the ceiling allow light to stream through in places. The stone sand beneath her feet has hardened over several millennia. There is another tunnel, flanked by two engravings, each the mirror-image of the other. Two men tearing out the heart of a creature with their bare hands. The men have one eye each in the centre of their foreheads. At the entrance to the tunnel there is a deep handprint, elongated and malformed. She puts her hand inside it. It is not the print of a single creature, but the gradual erosion, one hand at a time, of each hesitant visitor pausing at the edge of darkness.

The tunnel winds through the stone. It divides and splits and turns back on itself but Ghost Eye never hesitates. She knows it well. The noise of the water overwhelms all other sounds. It is too loud to be ignored.

THE CARNIVAL WAS STILL THERE when the soldier arrived at the next town over. Obediah Crow had some demands, easily accommodated, and when he said he would do it the rest of the carnies fell into line. He did his show that night and was gone by morning, on his way to New Badwater.

∞

I saw them preparing to leave. The last of the white folks' skins had cured and their flesh was salted and hung out to dry and tents were taken down and rolled up and piled onto the backs of mules.

They came to get me last.

I went willingly. Lured them into a false confidence.

I watched their supplies dwindling, saw that each night by the campfire the hunters returned with less and less. Knew it was time.

At night they tied my hands behind my back, bound my feet and tied them both together tightly. I'd lie on my side like a foetus till morning when they'd loosen the rope around my feet and untie it from my hands so I could shuffle behind them.

I wondered what they would eat first? A leg would have provided a decent helping but I would have struggled walking. I certainly could not have escaped if they had! An arm wouldn't provide as much but at least I'd be able to walk. I supposed they would go for my arms first. Then my legs, one at a time, when they had to. Then they'd throw me limbless over the back of a horse. The rest of me they would keep until they absolutely needed it, then they'd butcher me, turn me into jerky, sausages, blood pudding . . .

I was right. They came for my arm.

What did you do, Obediah?

See, the thing is . . . Remember how I told you my hands were bound together?

So when this big fucker comes over to cut one of my arms off—

What did you do, Obediah?
Did you headbutt him and take his knife?

He didn't use a knife.

Didn't use a knife.
Well what did he use?

A tomahawk.

A tomahawk?
It's like a hatchet.

He used a tomahawk. Held my arms out straight and swung hard as he could, right here . . .

∞

Obediah Crow made a chopping motion with his right

hand just above the elbow of his left hand.

∞

Took him a couple of swings but he got there.

He didn't!

He sure did. Then he got a bit of rope and tied it round my arm and twisted it round a stick. Then he turned the stick and kept turning it—now this hurt more than losing the damn arm—kept turning and turning till the blood stopped coming out the stump.

∞

With his right hand Obediah Crow rolled up his left sleeve. Then he took his gloves off, let the audience see the prosthetic.

They gasped.

Obediah smiled and slapped his thigh with his real hand.

∞

You know what I'd really like is to be able to take off the prosthetic and have a real hand beneath that. Now <u>that</u> would be some trick.

∞

The soldier had heard it already but he laughed all the

same. He slipped out before the end and rode back to the bathhouse, see if he could catch his lover when her shift was over.

Ghost Eye emerges halfway up the wall of an enormous cavern. She can see the level of the recent water on the walls above the height of the tunnel. The walls are still wet. The water only recently receded. A black and starless river runs through the floor of the long cave. Shafts of light from cracks in the rock are reflected in the black water forever. Red tendrils line the walls, so slow moving no human has ever seen them grow, but they have reached the roof of the chamber.

Stairs cut into the rock take her to the edge. Tiny white creatures swim away but return curiously as she splashes through the water, following the river through the rock. She feels it tug at her feet, though the surface appears still, trying to pull her under. She fights the desire to let it take her. If she drank from it, would she forget? Or would she die? Or worse: would she remember more than she cared to?

∞

There is a body floating face down in the water. She turns it over. Its one-eye is missing, the socket empty. She finds the others, bloated and eaten. There is no waterline here. The cave would have been filled. They waited too long, too frightened to emerge. Not scared of facing their hunters but of giving away their hiding place.

The swollen husks of the two Johns sit side by side, legs entwined, with their backs to the wall. All she had wanted was to rob their place, steal some food, a little money if they had it, but they caught her and invited her to stay. They seemed to be expecting her to ask about them but she never did, and the hand one John placed on the lower back of the other when they danced around one another whilst making dinner in the small kitchen, the tickle on the palm of the hand when they passed each other in the doorway, soon became open signs of affection for one another, legs pretzelled together as they shared a seat, kissing.

She was with them several months and helped around the small home, cooking stews and baking bread and hunting with the two Johns, one of whom was older than the other, his brown hair flecked grey at the sides. He was a painter and his work decorated the inside of the cabin. Now and again he would venture out to the bigger towns with several finished works to sell, and he got the odd commission for portraits, woodcuts, illustrations for children's books. The other John had red hair and a pointed little beard and was fond of a drink. They both were. He was a poet and musician, which was how the men spent their free time. They traded what they had with the Indians. Their pants and vests were decorated with thin white stripes that on close inspection were made up of tiny white dots painted on by hand.

Then one day the law came for the two men who had been found guilty of minding their own damned business. The Marshall threw a rope around young John's neck and dragged him behind the horse. When Aoife shot the horse and the lawman in quick succession, the men he had brought with him gave up the fight. The older John went to check on his lover while Aoife kept her shotgun on their attackers. The Marshall was still alive but the contents of his head were leaking out and his legs were trapped underneath his horse. Young John was alright, though the rope burn around his neck left a gnarled twisting scar, which he kept hidden by a purple cravat that now floated in the water.

She hears a noise from further up the tunnel, past the altar. Low voices or growls, the scraping of rock, some splashing in the water. She knows who it is. Where there is carnage, bodies, decay, they are there. She has seen them, naked, stalking burnt-out settlements, smearing ash on their faces and chewing on limbs still smoldering, drinking piss and fucking anything that still had skin. They see her and come closer. They are stooped, their legs bent, their arms hanging low, but not crawling. Wooden crosses dangle from leather string around their neck. They sniff the air. Their hair and beards are long and twisted and dirty, decorated with bones and buttons and twists of metal and strips of faded indigo cloth. There are four or five of them but they whistle, which echoes in the caves, to alert others. There is always more of them. Carrion crawlers. Parasites.

One of them comes closer, wary at first, fascinated by her skin. He reaches out to touch her black leather hand, runs a finger across the stitching, but Ghost Eye bats him away and he skitters backwards across the stone, his hands raised in apology. He bows. The others quickly move behind him, their heads bowed as well. They are fearful of her.

The man reaches behind his back.

Ghost Eye puts a hand on her pistol.

The man holds up one hand and with the other slowly brings out a knife from the belt around his waist. It is all he wears. His white body, like the others, is smeared with grey ash.

She lifts the gun from its holster and cocks the trigger.

Still holding the knife the man holds up his hands and sits down on a rock. He stretches one leg out in front of him and begins to hack it off. His face is that of a saint's tied to a burning stake—a mixture of agony and ecstasy. The others only look at Ghost Eye. When he has hacked away the flesh he begins to saw through the bone, hitting it with the handle of the knife to break it. When he is finished, he drops the knife and picks up the leg and offers it to her with his head low and his eyes closed. Blood spurts from the stump, trickles from the dead limb.

She watches as he bleeds out, his offering held aloft.

He opens his eyes. He does not make a sound but she can see him pleading. He picks up the knife and plucks out an eye but she does not acknowledge this. He sticks out his tongue and holds it and cuts through it to be mute like she is and when he dies soundlessly his companions set upon him and pull him apart with their fingers. They make room for her to join them but she ignores them.

THE CARNIES WERE SEVERAL days getting there but they set up shop quickly. There was a tent for the circus show, the acrobats, magician, another one for the moving pictures—everyone fascinated by the machine. *It's called a projector*, said the bowler-hat-wearing man who operated it. *The film goes in here*, he said, having to explain what film is. *I shine a light through the film and this*, he said, pointing at the little glass window at the front of the contraption, *is where the picture comes out. A little shutter opening and closing twenty-four times a second between each frame, or picture. Ma'am, please don't touch that ma'am. This one I made myself using the mechanism from a sewing machine*, spooling the film through the projector by hand at the correct speed—there was a booth selling cotton candy, another one selling kettle corn, corndogs, spruce beer, pretzels, taffy, a helter-skelter, a big wheel, and something none of them had ever seen before outside the mines: a gravity road. Four or five mine carts coupled together, with benches inside to sit on, that passengers rode down a narrow railway balanced precariously on a wooden structure, hauled by chains to the top and dropped down the other side and going up and round and down and over and under itself, coasting till it got back to the start, where the passengers would jump off and the next lot would get on. The gravity road took the longest to set up but there were folks queuing the entire time. For days families would be sure to have at least one member keeping them a place. And when they got off, they would rejoin the back of the queue and wait sometimes several hours to ride again.

∞

Obediah Crow set himself up in the hotel lobby. A stool on stage and a little table for his drink. When he wasn't performing he would be at the bar repeating the performance for smaller groups of patrons in exchange for drinks, or he couldn't be found. There was a room for him in the hotel but as far as anyone knew he was never there. Nobody saw him going in or coming out or even taking the stairs. There for a week and he never even took a bath.

I prefer to bathe outdoors, he'd say. *Smell me. Clean as a baby.*

My baby smells like sour-milk and shit.
That's your wife you're talking about!
Haw-haw-haw.

She navigates the tunnels and chambers of the shadow world, ignoring the art on the walls that once mesmerised her: the carving of a man disappearing into a wall like he was walking through it, which she used to sleep beside in the early days of the gang, back when it was only her and the boys. She is a ghost, Ghost Eye, emerging from the ground and lurking in shadows, glimpsed out the corner of an eye and gone at the turn of a head, a broken specter lurching from caves like a cyclops from the forge.

THE MORNING OF THE CEILIDH was spent getting ready—Sunday best, frocks, polished shoes, coats and vests and ties and shirts buttoned to the top and hats if you had them, hair combed if you didn't, bonnets, gloves up to the elbows, stockings . . . By lunchtime everyone was shitfaced, tucking into rye bread and scones and cakes and corn dogs and kettlecorn and candy floss and moonshine and steam beer and the combination of fried food and vomit was both appetising and off-putting, and the dogs came sniffing and the rats nobody knew were there rustled through half-eaten candy apples and fried potatoes and chunks of bread moist with mustard and regurgitated pretzels, and the rollercoaster ran endlessly, barely stopping to let people off and on, their sick spraying through the air on the tightest bends and the steepest drops, and nobody cared, whooping with glee and ducking spew or doing a little dance to keep their shoes clean but nobody saying nothing to anyone about it—it had been a whiles since they'd had a good knees up.

They had retreated into their homes in shame when they'd burned down the sheriff's office. How many folk had died that night? There was the sheriff, the deputy, the doctor, Ghost Eye . . . *Can't even remember now what it was Ghost Eye had done that was so bad* . . . Oh and there was Earl's daughter. Nobody knew where she got to. Earl swore blind it was Ghost Eye that did it, said he—*she*—had mystical powers and must've done it as revenge, even before we killed him—*her*—but everyone else knew that was hokum and he went mad raving to no-one about it and was found dead hanging by garters from the balcony above the piano—

AT THE CENOTE SHE STOPS. The pool before her is not emerald or turquoise but brown, nearly black. Detritus floats on the surface, clings to the walls, shards of glass, coils of metal covered in lichen. Broken shovel heads and saws and axe-handles protrude from the water. She looks at these things first, keeping her eyes off the island in the middle of the small pool, the mound of different-sized bodies pushed in from above, those of young children and of the burliest men, the rotten limbs scattered seem tossed in casually. Hand and footholds had been cut into the walls and she uses them to climb out of the sinkhole. Once hidden in the brush she sees now that this has been cleared. Stumps frame a wide path strewn with animal bones, useless tools and scraps of food and clothing. The path is well-trodden and carved with the grooves of barrow wheels. It winds a short distance into a small town. It is daylight but the town is quiet. She scans the fields for workers but these are empty. The rye stands tall, unharvested for a season, dusted white with ergot spores.

∞

At first she is wary of being seen but soon realises there is nobody there to see her. The streets are empty. Dried horse shit returned to straw blown everywhere by the wind. The shop doors lie open. She ventures inside the bank, the chemist, the saloon—all empty.

She continues through the ghost town, wondering what happened. A raid? Gunfight? Plague? She has a strong inclination that it is she who is out of place, that she got turned upside down in the underland and emerged not into the earthly realm but the underworld.

Maybe I died after all, she mutters aloud.

She sees the church, its doors and windows boarded up, the grounds strewn with hastily constructed crosses. Round back is one big cross, two branches lashed together with rope that's since gone slack so it makes more of a crooked X instead of a crucifix; before it a huge mound of dirt.

∞

She does not notice the people at first, then when she does, she thinks they are dead, with their skin pulled taut against their skulls grey and mottled, slack jaws, unmoving. They sit on their porches, stare out of windows. None of them move more than their eyes or a dizzy swivelling of a head on the stalk of a neck. It is not something she notices right away but each one is missing a limb. They watch her, this shadow, a black apparition, moving through their town. They have been awaiting her, death, and they are ready. But Ghost Eye is not here for them. She is sorry for whatever curse has been brought upon them, even though they likely brought it down upon their selves and their children.

She follows the black hole in the sky.

BY EVENING TIME when the ceilidh was supposed to start, boys and girls were swinging from the top of the big wheel and a magician had sawn a volunteer in half and fucked it up and the blood was spraying and the man from the audience was screaming and the saw, when it was pulled out the box with a flourish and the cross section revealed, flung giblets into the audience, who whistled and hollered thinking it was part of the act, clapping at the meat falling from the box, the dead legs at one end and the anguished face with tongue lolling out the mouth at the other, wondering how it was done, the magician wiping blood from his face and grinning, taking a bow, soaking up the blood and applause. In the cinema tent the audience jostled for position at the front to see the train pulling into station and they all screamed as it came towards the camera but it didn't stop and came hurtling through the screen and they clambered over one another to get away from it, pulling hair, fingers in mouths, in eyes, elbows in cheeks, foots on faces squished to the floor, more than fifty of them trying to squeeze out the single exit at the back of the tent blocked by the projectionist's equipment, pushing it over so the train was falling from the ceiling, everyone scratching and dancing and spraying foam from between clenched teeth— And over in the saloon where the band had been practising, just below where Earl had dropped and broke his neck and shat all over the piano, the chairs and tables had been pushed to the side as though for a wedding dance, the ceilidh was in full swing, the willow being stripped, dancers birlin each other around, kicking and spinning and swapping partners, faces red and sweating and smiling and singing and belting out instructions, nobody knowing the dance when the name was given— *Dashing White Sergeant—How's that one go?—Gay Gordons—I like this one but I cannae mind it*—But it all came back to them like shagging when they got started, only half-remembering, being pure shite but giving it all ye've got being more than half the fun—

∞

And meanwhile, over in the hotel lobby, Obediah Crow was halfway through the Dismantled Man—

∞

Remember how I said my hands were bound together? Well now one of those hands wasn't attached to my body. So while the savage was tying off my stump I worked my other hand free. My dead hand was still warm. I curled up the fingers of it into a fist. Then I held onto the elbow. When the savage stepped back to inspect his work I sprung to my feet—

∞

Obediah Crow leapt up from his stool and stood with his legs apart, his left arm hanging limp by his side but his right arm pulled back over his shoulder like he was about to swing an axe.

∞

And I swung my dead hand at him hard as I could. Got him right in the temple. He stayed standing for what must have been a minute or so. Long enough for me to see his eyeballs fill with red, blood trickle from his nose, his ear. Could see the outlines of the broken bones sticking through the skin at the side of his face. Then he keeled over.

I stood over him. He had a knife, which I used to untie my feet. I took his tomahawk too. Still have it.

∞

The audience edged forwards in their seats to see it, the ones at the back standing up, no-one really able to see much at all, the lanterns around the stage lighting up the inside of their eyeballs, floating black dots of protein swimming, Obediah Crow's dead hand moving much like a real one . . .

The boys and girls on the big wheel trying to rock it off its hinges—*Let's roll this thing down mainstreet!*—cheered on by its operator . . .

The cinema tent collapsing in on itself, the skewed image of the phantom train engulfing them in warped black and white, the audience wriggling inside the canvas like larva, their hands and legs no longer working, chewing through the inside of their faces trying to get out—

∞

Obediah Crow reached behind him and took the tomahawk out of his belt. He lifted the leg of his trousers to show the knife strapped to his shin.

∞

But do you know what? I rather liked my hand. In a way I preferred it more dead than I did alive. My hand had become a weapon. When another one came to see what was happening—after all, I had stopped screaming and they were all waiting for my arm to be brought back to the campfire and cooked—I clocked him with my dead hand as well. This one dropped but didn't die right away. Took a few more swings of the dead hand—busted up his nose and his eyes and most of his teeth but he still groaned and twitched so I stomped on him a few times.

I snuck around the back of the tents to the horses and untied one. Then I stopped. I was in a hurry to get away, don't get me wrong, but I had to be smart. I was fat enough to live off my reserves for a while but them mountains were far away and I needed my strength. I couldn't survive just by eating myself from the inside out.

But I had my hand. And I'd acquired a taste for white meat.

∞

And inside the saloon the ceilidh dancers lurched into one another, kicking and swinging and twisting wrists until arms pulled clean off with a pop from shoulder sockets like the limbs of cheap dolls, kicking at shins till the shins bled and toes mashed to a pulp, the fiddler's fingers cut through to the bones, his bow a mess of torn hair, the guitarist's nails hanging off, knuckles blistered and burst and blistered again, the pianist hammering at the ivory with his fists curled up like someone wounded in the war, eyes open wide and staring, mouths open drooling, trembling shaking dancing . . .

∞

That would see me through one night.

If I could get a fire going.

But it got me thinking.

I took out the knife I'd stolen from the one who took my arm. I crept on my tiptoes towards one of the tents.

There were little ones in the group. Less likely to put up a fight. So I cut a hole in the back of the tent.

The women, I knew, were tending to the fire, the men were

waiting. Soon they would be looking for me. Maybe some of them already were.

∞

Nobody saw Ghost Eye scuttling between buildings, the black leather of her skin creaking and squeaking disguised by the noise of the party, and those who did see her, the hairless black shadow, one white-red eye staring hard and one black shiny one reflecting the white of the moon, looking for *him,* the one who'd done it, who'd been doing it all along.

She had found another outside of town. Fresh. Tied to a boulder, tourniquet below the knee, nothing below that . . . The remains of a fire. She did not have the heart to dig through the ash. She knew what she would find there. The girl had died. He might get another meal out of her before she turned bad, but he'd likely have to take another one.

∞

Inside the tent were several little ones, all asleep. I lifted a girl, must've been around five or six, still in her sleeping sack. I whispered a few things in her ear and stroked her hair and held her against my chest with my one arm.

∞

She had known about him for a while. Impossible not

to. Ghost Eye's posters had hung beside those of missing kids often enough that she had tried to stay aware of what happened, if only to keep the law off her back. But that one agent . . . seemed to think a gang of train robbers who had never so much as killed anybody by mistake might also fuck and eat kids . . .

∞

It wasn't easy to get us both onto the horse with one arm but I managed. By the time they started shooting at us we were out of range.

∞

The first girl'd gone missing in the February, snatched during the night by Injuns, they said, which didn't make much sense since the girl was Indian or at least half-a-one—her father getting her mother pregnant on one of the nights they snuck off together and a marriage quickly arranged for them—though they didn't resist being in love and all—by the chief of her mother's tribe and the foreman of the railroad construction firm for whom her pa worked. Searches were, at first, vigorous but unfruitful, with all available folk searching day and night, calling the girl's name, knocking on doors, ransacking camps, pinning up posters that offered handsome and ever-increasing rewards, but then folk had to go back to work and the wives had to tend to their chores so searching was relegated to night time only, and then someone suggested, and the rest of them talked themselves into agreeing with their assessment of the situation, that it was the Injuns't done it and were likely long gone now and the searching stopped completely except for an agent, who'd come to know the folk working on the railroads, having shot or apprehended many of the bandits responsible for robbing the people and the cargo that rode upon them, who'd been on the trail of one particular gang for some time now and who were said to've been nearby—robbed a train 's a matter of fact—when the girl got disappeared, and not staying in one town for any longer than a single night, arriving late and leaving first thing (and only then when he was in absolute dire need of a bath or a change of clothes, preferring as he did to camp out on his own or with the Injuns or railroad workers when he desired a little company or had a little dried meat to trade for tobacco) therefore missed—on numerous occasions—the stories of the mountain man who'd claimed to have killed more than a thousand natives, eating all or part of at least a few dozen, at first only when desperate and then, having acquired the taste, like one does with olives or anchovies or the baby-vomit smell of blue cheese, would deliberately hunt, salt and smoke as much of it that he'd need for his travels, trade some of it as jerky along the way and trying not to laugh as he did so, including—he'd claim—four-and-twenty Indian girls, a number that'd increase over subsequent tellings, and could be attributed to exaggeration, though the audience knew that good storytelling had at least some basis in the truth and just enough embellishment to make it worth listenin' to, it was just as likely that he ate more'n'more kids as he made his way 'cross the country telling stories of his time as a sailor, soldier, log cabin builder, fur trader, carpenter, and which was, if truth be told, more or less what happened.

∞

In the saloon the dancers spun and bared teeth and locked lips and teeth and chewed through tongues and the pianist pummeled his hands atonally to paste on the splintered white keys, the wire of the jaw-harp poking through the lips of its handler like some metal insect biting its prey, the stringed instruments silent, the strings having cut through digits though the players kept playing on, ghost sounds, grace notes, only the hammering of the piano keys keeping rhythm for the dancers getting faster getting faster—

∞

She was my first Indian. I soon found a liking for the taste. I've since killed and eaten many of them. In the hundreds probably.
   Including the one I was married to.

∞

Kicking and spinning and laughing and shouting and

counting and swapping and slapping and kicking and clapping and spinning and twisting and digging clawed hands into wrists and down arms and curls of skin spiraling to the floor like whittlings—

∞

Nobody misses them. They're like a blight. And I'm a cull.

∞

The pianist's bloodied fists a blurry arc pounding the keys, the dancers pulling at one another, ripping off clothes and wrenching off limbs and kicking shins through to bones and stamping on hands and arms and faces, scratching themselves raw and chewing through tongues and cheekskin, chucking chairs and tables and smashing glasses and bottles, throwing them in the air, into faces, spitting and vomiting, clutching seized stomachs, open sores erupting on their faces, arms, chests and bellies, dresses ripped and trousers unbuckled and spit and semen and blood and shit and vomit and booze and chicken wings and ribs . . . and the piano keys break and splinter and bury themselves into the pulp of the pianist's hands till he cannot go any longer, and the dancers spin themselves around and kick their legs off like rainboots and collapse lifeless and limbless onto the floor—

∞

And Ghost Eye emerges from the shadows behind Obediah Crow as he drains his glass in one long pull and when he sets it down again on the small table beside his tool she opens him up from ear to ear so the bottom of his face flaps open and peels away, a macabre smile, a puzzled expression, but she had not simply cut him, she had dug the knife in deep and his mouth filled with bone dust and his teeth slackened and the bottom part of his jaw hinged open and dropped into his lap, fumbled at by his dead hand, his tongue without a mouth to rest inside flopping out like some hideous necktie. She tosses the knife into the audience and vanishes.

∞

Applause.

fade to black & white

AOIFE CLIMBS ABOARD the final carriage as it leaves the station, pulls her hat down low, and takes a seat at the back. She keeps her hands hidden in her pockets and rests her head on the cold window. She might have slept but the difference between waking and sleeping is indistinguishable to her now. The train is swallowed by a hole blasted through the mountains.

When she opens her eyes, the carriage is empty. Condensation steams from her mouth but she does not feel the cold. The window is clouded. She wipes it with her leather hand. Behind it is all white. She peers through the fog, sees only occasional shapes—a branch, a stone, maybe a break in the mountains, the outline of a valley, a vague landscape drawn in a few strokes of washed ink.

The leather of her hand is cracked, torn in places, worn smooth in others. The skin on the side of a finger flaps open. She folds it down and holds it in place with the adjacent finger.

The train turns.

She can see the front carriages out the windows opposite. She shuffles across the aisle and sits down, puts her forehead against the window. The front of the train is hidden by its own steam. She can clearly see the carriages ahead. Through the foggy windows she should be able to see movement, outlines of faces, maybe even be able to hear them over the noise of the wheels on the track. Surely she is not the only person on the train.

She pulls herself through the carriage using the seats on either side, though she does not yet need the support. She hauls the carriage door open. A rush of cold air hits her lungs. She reaches out and pulls open the door of the next carriage and hops across the gap. She leaves the door open behind her. There is nobody to complain about the noise or the drop in temperature. Not even a hat or bag or forgotten coat or discarded ticket stub or empty bottle kicked beneath a seat.

She wanders the rest of the immaculate carriages. All are the same. Empty. Everybody gone. She sits down on the first seat of the front carriage. There is no front door to this one. The only doors are the ones at the side, for the platforms. Instead of a front door to get into the next carriage there is an oil painting of a locomotive—this one?—crossing the plains and a chair for the conductor. No sign of him either.

Surprised he didn't take the damn chair too.

The train turns again. She can see the locomotive ahead, a corner of the tender too, but cannot see into the cab for the smoke and steam.

Outside is all white. Still. The train snakes through

cloud. The locomotive appears sometimes in the left window, sometimes the right. The rest of the time it ploughs on straight ahead at a constant speed.

She must have slept.

When she opens her eyes the locomotive is out the window across the aisle, pointing in almost the opposite direction. She walks the length of the carriage, looks out each window in turn, trying to see into the cab, see if she can signal to the driver. She enters the next carriage, then the next, trying to keep level with the cab, trying to see in, until she comes to the final one just as it reaches the turning, and she finds herself staring out the back door at nothing. White. Oblivion.

She opens the rear door. The tracks beneath her blink out after a couple of yards. She grips the handle. Looks down. She sees her reflection, distorted but still, between the sleepers. It has been a long time since she has seen herself. She looks more or less like she imagines. The train rises and falls like a ship, like the tracks have been laid across water. But the water is solid.

She remains there for a moment. Then she turns and lunges through the carriages. When she reaches the one at the front she wrenches open the door. She braces herself against the frame like she is about to hurl herself out into the void. She leans out, looks forwards, then up and around. She hangs onto the door handle and manoeuvres outside.

She inches along the outside of the carriage and around it until she is over the coupling. The tender is full. She pulls herself onto it, kicking coal onto the track, tearing the leather of her knees.

The driver's cab is empty. The furnace is still burning. She has stolen from many trains but has never stolen one. Outside, she still cannot see anything. The train carries on its invisible route. She tries the handles, the levers, not knowing what she is doing, but nothing happens. The coal in the fire never seems to burn out though she does not add any more to it. There is a bucket of water.

The train slows to a stop.

She gets off, starts her journey across the ice. The world below is clearer but upside down, as though through a pinhole camera. It is here where she sees the figure in the mist before her. She follows it. She does not want to be found, she just wants a way out. She follows the figure like a shadow, not thinking of it as a person but a path. Every now and then it stops, turns around. She remembers doing this. But the feeling of being followed stopped being useful to her a long time ago.

Inverted beneath the ice she sees the others. She looks up. They are in a line, a human train, a procession. Their feet do not touch the ice. They appear to be held up by the collars of their death garb, suspended in the air, toes pointing downwards. She falls in behind them but they soon depart. She cannot keep up. She is stuck in a different loop to the others.

The one she is following stops again.

She stops too but does not make any effort not to

be seen.

The one she is following lights a fire.

She crawls towards it. She cannot feel its warmth but is drawn towards it nonetheless. It is the only colour she has seen since leaving the train.

The one she is following is lying on the ground. They turn over, see their follower, their ghost. They see the foliage that sprouts from its leather pores, the curls of dry leaves and green-brown flecks of moss that fall from it as it speaks, one eye hidden, the other made of stone.

'Lo there, they say, and invite her to sit.

END.

The Badwater Trilogy

The Philistines Be Upon Thee
But God Made Hell
Cyclops from the Forge

With thanks always to my family, to my editor, Euan, for his continual encouragement, enthusiasm and suggestions, to Alex, Kev, *Hedera Felix*, my work-fam, and everybody else who helped and supported these books in some way.

'Rattlesnake Shake' and 'Desert of Glue' are both titles of songs by Wolf Eyes, whose album *Dread* was essential listening when writing this book.

Ghost Eye Seeker is an album by Crow Tongue.

MALKI PRESS
EDINBURGH

Malkipress.weebly.com
malkipressedinburgh@gmail.com
@malkipress

Also available from Malki Press:

A Girl in a Pool; Detritus & Brux by Euan McBride

A Knife Fight in the Front Garden by Louise Meldrum

Printed in Great Britain
by Amazon